Deja Vou- All Over Again

May your memories be memorable, Blessings & Love

Darlene Link

Darlene Link

authorHOUSE®

2018

AuthorHouse™
1663 Liberty Drive, Suite 200
Bloomington, IN 47403
www.authorhouse.com
Phone: 1-800-839-8640

First published by AuthorHouse   2/28/2008

ISBN: 978-1-4259-4367-7 (sc)

Library of Congress Control Number: 2006905296

Printed in the United States of America
Bloomington, Indiana

This book is printed on acid-free paper.

PREFACE

DEJA VOU - ALL OVER AGAIN is the love story of two mature adults who meet again after thirty-five years. Getting reacquainted, they share memories they were sure the other would never remember. But there is more than just the past that attracts them to each other. There is the wonder that, at their age anyone could have feelings and emotions they believed until now were only experienced by the young.

Deb Sullivan is content with her single life now, having raised a family during a difficult marriage that would have ended in divorce had her husband, Dan not died.

Glen Jarvis believed during his eight years as a widower he would never love again. Now as they share memories of their past, they are drawn by a chemistry between them. Each is impressed with the other's depth of faith in God and how naturally they express it. They treasure family and friends who share their lives.

Before they allow themselves to love each other completely, there are shadows from their separate pasts they want to deal with. To find happiness together in the years they have left is a risk they have to consider. Amazingly, the risk seems easier now than when they were younger.

This story will appeal to all ages, since we often believe that days of love and sex, passion and romance will fade as we grow older, though there is the hope that love is ageless. Writing this story gave me gave an opportunity to use my writing skills and vicariously tell the story of Deb and Glen. Darlene D. Link

❧ CHAPTER 1 ❧

THE PHONE WAS RINGING AS SHE unlocked the door. Dropping her purse on the sofa, she hurried to catch it before the machine did. "Hello?"

A male voice spoke. "Hello, is this Deb Sullivan?"

"Yes" She said trying to recognize the voice.

"This is Glen. Did you get my message?" *I can hear my pulse in my ear. I have to concentrate to hear above the pounding in my head. Why am I so nervous?*

"Message?" She asked. "What message? I don't, oh, I'm sorry, I just walked in the door as the phone was ringing. I haven't."

He interrupted, "then you don't know." He stopped to swallow. "This is Glen, Glen Jarvis. Do you remember me? Do you remember Chris Jarvis? Chris and Connie, I'm Chris' brother. They used to live in Mallory when you did. He was a teacher and coach there. Well, I ah," he ran out of words and breath at the same time.

"Yes, I remember you," she searched her memory. "I'm

surprised, though, to hear from you. It must be a hundred years."

"Close," he agreed and relaxed a bit. "Well, I was talking to Connie, my sister-in-law a couple of weeks ago. She is still in touch with Mildred Evans. Mildred sent her a newspaper article over a year ago telling of Dr. Sullivan's death. Mildred knew that you still live here in Grand Island."

"Yes."

"When I told Connie I was coming to Grand Island, she told me about Doctor Sullivan and suggested I call you." He explained. *I'm talking too much rambling on.* "Ah, how are you doing?"

"I'm, well, I'm doing just fine, Glen."

"I hope it's okay if I call you, now, I mean." He wondered why he said that.

"Well, of course it's, it's fine. I'm glad you called. Did you say you are here in Grand Island?" Deb tried to put it all together.

"Oh yeah, you haven't listened to your messages so I'd better tell you. I planned to come to Grand Island on business and Connie encouraged me to call you" he tried to explain. "Anyway, I'm here at the Holiday Inn. I left the message on your machine this morning and hoped you'd call me back, but I didn't wait." He stopped.

It was Deb's turn. "I.just got home." Her mind racing, she thought of asking him over for coffee or something when he spoke again.

"I thought we could meet for lunch, but how about coffee this afternoon or a drink this evening."

"Yes, coffee, but it has to be a bit later this afternoon. I have several calls to make and then I'm free. Well, I'm really not free. It might cost you, for the coffee." She joked.

He laughed. "Okay, just tell me where and when."

"Since you are at the Holiday Inn, I could meet you there in the coffee shop at, oh, three. Is that okay?"

"That's fine but it's not out of your way?" He asked.

"No problem." She assured him. "See you at three." *I wonder why I'm in such a hurry to hang up.*

"Wait!" He called."Will I? How will I know you?"

"Oh, well, I'm almost as tall as I was and my hair is whiter now. And I'm wearing a navy blazer among other things." He laughed, a pleasant laugh. *What a brilliant thing to say, off to a great start* Deb scolded herself.

"Me too. I mean, almost as tall as I was. My hair is gray what I have left of it." Now they both laughed. "Well, we'll find each other. I'd better let you go."

"Yes, okay, bye." Deb hung up. "Wow." She heard herself say out loud. Stopping at her desk in the office, *it's been at least thirty years since I've seen him. I thought about him a few times over the years though, well maybe more than a few times, but it's been a long time.*

She pushed the button on the answering machine. There were four messages. One was from the church telling her the name of a lady in the hospital who would have emergency bypass tonight. Deb needed to see her this afternoon. Another was a friend, Wilma who was in town shopping and wanted to meet for lunch."I guess I missed you this time so will try again next time." Then a click.

The third call was from Deb's daughter, Peggy who lives here in Grand Island. She was inviting her mom to dinner. *Peg and I have an understanding, since we live so close. We invite each other over often but feel free to say "no" without offense.* Deb called her number and left a message saying not to count on her tonight. She didn't say why or that she may be busy. It all depends on how the coffee date turns out.

Then there was Glen's message. It said "Deb, Deb Sullivan, this is Glen Jarvis. I don't know if you remember me. I'm Chris Jarvis' brother. We met while you lived in Mallory. Well, I'm in Grand Island. I thought you might meet me for lunch or something. Call me here at the Holiday Inn if you want to." He left the hotel and his cell number. Then he repeated them. Deb pushed the save button and went into her bedroom. In front of the mirror, she peered at her face wondering what Glen would think of what stared back at her. There were some lines that had come sneaking in over the years. She shrugged and touched up a few spots with makeup and ran a comb though her unruly white hair.

Glen Jarvis, the first time she met him, she still remembers. He was so tall, his head could almost scrape the ceiling and he had to duck through the doorway in Chris and Connie's house.

In the kitchen, Deb cut off a slice of cheese from a chunk of cheddar and took out a couple of wheat crackers, poured half a glass of milk and drank it down. Grabbing an apple from the drawer in the fridge she reminded herself of her resolve to always sit down to eat when she became single. So she sat down and called her best friend, Eileen. She shared her recent news with her. Eileen was excited for her and said to call her back when she could even if it were late. She wanted the details. "I've got to go now. Talk to you later." They hung up.

She pulled the door shut and with a few strides, slid into the driver's seat of her van. *I remember when we moved to Mallory some forty years ago. We quickly became friends with a group of people who were mostly our age. Some were single and others married. They were teachers, farmers and merchants in the community, some lifelong, others like us were new to the area. We were especially welcome though because Dan was the handsome, young brilliant new doctor in town.*

They liked me because I was a typical doctor's wife. I never figured out what that meant. I was tall and stately and had several toddlers in tow most of the time. We were informed soon after arriving that we would have certain friends and belong to organizations and activities that were proper for us. We were to do business locally if possible and never go to the local saloons.

Dan was more concerned with his image than I. He managed to do his thing secretly and/or out of town. I was friendly to everyone, not just the elite and willing to be involved in community causes. Mostly I chose to live my life as a mom and wife and mind my own business. Gossip was a favorite activity and we were a favorite topic. I purposely knew nothing.

The locals were cliquish preferring original residents. As small towns go, you were really only accepted if you are third or fourth generation residents or marry one of them. However, since they knew your business, they were quick to come to the rescue if you needed something.

Our circle of friends was diverse and most were like us, new in town. We had local sports and community events in common. We also had drinking alcohol and eating in common. We partied a lot. After local activities we partied at each other's houses. How we partied, was evident. We spent more money on booze than on food.

We had a yearly event, the state basketball tournament in Grand Island. We all hired babysitters and spent the weekend "in the city." We attended most of the games, no matter which teams were playing. There was also shopping, eating and partying. It kept us sane, living in a small town under the peering eyes of all. It was time out of the fish-bowl.

After a local basketball game when we were at Chris Jarvis'. Glen came to see his brother's team play and he showed up at Chris'. The guys were in the living room rehashing the evenings basketball game. We women were in the kitchen fixing snacks and chatting. Chris brought Glen into the kitchen to introduce him. I only remember that he had to duck to miss the archway. He said hello and went back to join the other guys. "Nice looking and tall!" I silently observed. I couldn't be blamed for noticing.

⚔ CHAPTER 2 ⚕

GLEN LAID THE PHONE ON THE table and leaned back on the pillows. He smiled. *Guess I didn't need to worry about whether Deb would remember me or her reception of my call after all. Cripes, I thought about it and practiced what to say enough while I drove up here.*

She was friendly before, why not now? Her voice sounded the same. He thought back, I remember when I first met her.

It was the first time I went to Mallory. Chris had a game that night and a houseful of people over after the game. He introduced me to the guys in the living room. They were doing a postmortem on the game. Then he took me into the kitchen to meet the women who were busy getting lunch ready, chatting and laughing.

I didn't remember anyone's name, but I did remember a tall and willowy woman who looked neat and attractive. She had an appealing laugh and jokingly invited me to help with the food, listing chores I could handle. I declined and she made some remark about women having to do everything. I assumed she was a teacher.

Later, I saw her leave with the doctor, but again I assumed what I

7

wanted, that they were just going together. It was wishful thinking. I thought they made a handsome couple, and I felt a twinge of envy.

The next time I met her was at the Elks Club in Madison. I wonder if she remembers. I was coming to spend the weekend with Chris and Connie and watch Mallory play in the district tournaments. Our crowd was going to have dinner afterward at the Elks. I was late so by the time I got there, they were in the bar at the Elks waiting to go into the dining room. That woman, the tall one, was there but the doctor wasn't. The guys offered me the chair right next to hers. They introduced themselves again. I remembered her name was Deb. We joked that we were both alone and that her date had stood her up. I was going to order a meal but Deb said she had ordered an extra T-bone steak for her "missing date". That's what she called him. I could have his steak if I didn't mind. I agreed and the table full of friends joked about my being her date if I was going to eat her steak. We all laughed and joked about it. When we went into the dining room, I sat in the chair next to her. She seemed a bit shy but was friendly. I know I flirted with her and she seemed not to mind. The group was playing it up so I played along and thought she did too.

After dinner, I even invited her to ride back to Mallory with me, since her date stood her up. She politely refused and rode back to Mallory with the Evan's. I figured she was embarrassed to accept a ride with all of those people there. What other reason could there be? She seemed to enjoy my company at dinner. Though she was like that to everyone. I knew I could like her a lot. Maybe she was serious about the doctor. Maybe not and she might go out with me.

Glen shook his head remembering how he felt even after all of these years. *I admit I thought of her more than once over the years, even after marrying Myrna. In fact, I couldn't help comparing Deb to other women. Why, I don't understand.*

Glen checked his watch. *I have a couple of hours until I meet her, might as well take a nap. It was so late when I got in last night.* He slipped off his shoes and lay back on the pillows. *Wonder what she looks like now. She was good-looking not exactly beautiful. Classy, striking would be the word, I guess, not showy. One of those women who looks good in anything, even jeans and a T-shirt. She carried herself well, gracefully. She always seemed aware and interested whether it was about a person or what was going on around her. She never missed a thing and there seemed to always be laughing and fun whenever she was present.* He shook his head again trying to describe her in his thoughts.

As she drove out of the yard, Deb remembered the last time she met Glen. *It was at the Elks Club in Madison. Dan had an emergency at the hospital at the last minute, so I rode to the game with Mildred and her husband, Jake. Dan hoped to get there for dinner at least so I ordered his favorite, a rare T-bone steak. He'd eat it sometime if he didn't show up tonight. I looked up and everyone was welcoming Glen Jarvis to join us. He took the empty chair next to me. He summoned the barmaid to order a drink and bring him a menu. I told him if he liked steak, he might as well eat Dan's. It didn't look like he was going to make it. As soon as Glen agreed, our friends teased that he would have to be my date if he was going to eat my steak. He agreed, but wondered if I would pay the tab. I said I would. Our whole crowd joked and teased us the rest of the evening.*

When we went into the dining room, they insisted my "date" should sit by me. I just put up with their joke. After dinner, Glen offered me a ride home. He reasoned that he would have to drive alone. I decided it would not be a good idea since I was married so I declined and went back with Mildred and Jake Evans.

I thought that was the end of it until the next day when Mildred called me. She couldn't wait to tell me that Glen had called her the day after the Elks dinner. He didn't know my last name and hoped she would give him my phone number. He was going to ask me for a date. She told him my name and number but said she wasn't sure I would go out with him.

"Is she serious about the doctor?" Glen asked.

"I guess you could say that," Mildred laughed. "She's his wife and they share some kids." I wonder if Glen remembers that. Why would he? It was too many years ago.

⚔ CHAPTER 3 ⚔

DEB JARRED HERSELF INTO THE PRESENT as she pulled into Gus and Inga Mitchell's driveway. It was time to remind herself that she had three calls to make before three o'clock. Her mind was hardly on pastoral care but she forced herself to shift into work mode, that of caring for these special people. Grabbing her bag from the seat next to her, it held a Bible, communion equipment and bulletins from Sunday worship to share with shut ins. Her attention had to focus on caring for Gus and Inga now, They were in their late eighties and seemed to take turns being care givers to each other. It was a matter of time before one or both of them would need elder or nursing home care.

It was hard to see these precious elders take giant steps backward. Their golden years of retirement seemed to quickly be replaced by failing eyesight and hearing loss. Other health problems added to their burden. Soon they would be unable to care for their homes or drive cars. Gus had driven until two weeks ago when he ran into a parked car across the street. He swung out too far as he turned into his driveway. It shook him into realizing he needed to give up driving even though it hurt a lot to do it. His car was still in the driveway with "For Sale" in the window. It was just another freedom and privilege he lost. Now he had to depend on others for things he had done for himself for sixty or seventy years.

Deb had only known most of these people since their active years were over. Her job as Visitation Chaplain was a connection to their church home. Gus and Inga had been active and faithful, even financially. Now they were unable to attend worship because of their fragile conditions. Deb brought them news of their friends and life in the congregation. Many of them were homebound too. It was easy to love each of them as if they were her own parents. Deb visited with her charges for a while and shared religious literature from the church. Then she'd serve them Holy Communion and share prayers. All of her senior people knew their Lord. Deb had to admit that she got more satisfaction from this job than she gave it. One only had to listen to become wiser.

Inga was especially confused today. She carried on her own conversation, telling Deb about how they ran the store and the huge garden they had and how many jars of beans and peas and carrots she canned every year. She talked about how hard she worked raising six kids in those days.

Gus ignored her story and carried on his own conversation about business in a small town. Deb loved stories of when the prairie was simple and people worked so hard. Sometimes, she heard the same story many times but they had a new twist and she would learn another detail. "It took the whole family to run the business." Gus repeated louder. "Why, we sold everything from gas to eggs and produce from the garden."

Each of them hardly heard what the other said and just talked louder if they weren't finished and the other one started Deb let them go on in the past while she prepared the elements for Holy Communion at the dining table. Then she called them both to come.

From the past she had learned not to let them read together. Inga would read fast and loud and Gus couldn't keep up, so he would get angry. Now, Inga read the Apostle's Creed and Gus read the Lord's Prayer. That way pleased both of them.

Gus saw Deb to the door and shook her hand thanking her for coming. He shared quietly that Inga was a bit confused today. Deb smiled as she turned away.

Deb stopped at the hospital to see the surgical member who had requested a pastoral call. Norma Franklin's family was waiting in the lounge. Norma's daughter, Flora told Deb that her mother was already in pre-op and would have a bypass and possibly a pace maker before the evening was over. The doctor had been there and told them there is always a risk but that he thought it would be quite routine and take several hours. They would get the doctor's report when it was over. Deb prayed with them for their mother's safe surgery and recovery. She included prayers for strength and faith of the family, whatever the outcome. Deb told the family that the prayer chain at church had been activated for their mother, Norma. They thanked her.

The next visit was to a lady Deb had learned to love, Vera

Sylvester. She had a lot of arthritic pain and spent most of her time in her tiny senior housing apartment. It was hot and stuffy to Deb, but Vera felt less pain if it was warm. Odors of spices and cooking mingled with stale, sweaty apartment air in the hallways.

Vera had given up her large home by the river when her husband died ten years before. She grieved one as much as the other. Her social life changed abruptly. To her, life ended. Her only son, Paul lived two hundred miles away and had a job that took all of his time. He called a lot but hardly ever came to visit. He wanted his mother to move to senior housing near him and it was inevitable soon.

Often Deb brought a fast food meal that they shared even though Vera had meals- on-wheels delivered. She loved hamburgers, greasy fries and frosties, gobbling it all down. She complained that the food from meals-on-wheels was tasteless and she was sure they had an overstock of corn which she couldn't eat.

Sometimes, Deb took her to her doctor's appointments or brought her flowers from the garden. Today, they just had tea together. She didn't notice Deb sneaking peeks at her watch so she'd be on time for her next appointment. Vera accepted Holy Communion and as usual she wept. Deb gave her a hug and set a date for their next visit posting it on Vera's fridge to help her remember. Deb could hardly wait to get out of there. The heat, the odors, but she had another reason to go.

At last, she could concentrate on her social life such as it was. There was the Baptist minister she met in CPE(Clinical Pastoral Education). They had coffee together when they met in the hospital while seeing patients. They often talked about religion and world problems that related to religion. Another man she met at aerobic class liked to go out for lunch or coffee with her after class but Deb realized he really wanted to dump his extended family's problems on her more than he wanted a date. At least with them, Deb was safely single. She got more nervous as she drove closer to the hotel and Glen.

⚔ CHAPTER 4 ⚕

GLEN FELT RESTED FROM HIS NAP. He freshened up, changing his shirt and left his room early, hoping she would be there. His thoughts raced. "*I should have asked her what her car looked like. Oh, well, I'll know her anyway. We didn't agree where to meet. What if she is already in the coffee shop? He looked there first.*

The lobby seemed dark so he stepped out into the sunlight. Then he saw Deb. It had to be Deb. A silver colored minivan pulled into a spot and a tall white-haired woman got out. She walked with the same stride he remembered. A purse was slung over her shoulder, she had on a navy jacket over a white blouse open at the neck. A light blue skirt made her look professional yet comfortable. "Just what I expected," he said to himself.

The woman looked up and they both smiled. Deb had a hard time walking straight with him watching her. He stepped out to meet her, extending his hand. It felt good taking hers. "Deb?" He asked though he knew.

"Glen, I hope." They laughed. "Good to see you again," as he turned to open the door.

"This is great!" He said, trying to stay calm. "I'd have known you anywhere. You haven't changed a bit."

"How long has it been since you had your eyes examined?" She teased looking up sideways at him. She'd forgotten how tall he really was.

The hostess seated them in a booth. A waitress brought a basket of popcorn and took their drink orders. They both passed up coffee for lemonade and sat back to relax.

"You do look just as I remember you, except for the white hair. It's very becoming to you, sort of like a halo." He said.

"Thank you. I've never been so glad to have white hair."

"Just be grateful you have hair, whatever the color." Glen patted the top of his head.

"I have a theory about that. It's not that a person loses his or her hair, it just grows in a different place like in their ears, up their nose or straight across the forehead and other places." She illustrated as she spoke.

Glen gave a robust laugh. "I'll try to remember that. It will give me comfort when I run the comb through less and less hair." He took a sip of his drink. "You said you had calls to make. Does that have anything to do with your professional look?"

"Yes, though I'm also supposed to look friendly. I do pastoral care and visitation to members of my congregation who are not able to attend church for whatever reason or just need someone to talk to."

"You're congregation? Does that mean you are a pastor?"

"No, I am a lay chaplain but I'm there to help the pastors."

"Sounds interesting but aren't these sick and dying people?

"Some are, yes. Most are old and lonely and not too happy about their life now or in their future."

"But isn't it depressing, a downer?"

"It can be sometimes but I have learned to love these people and they love me, even the crabby ones. Some have dementia, but I just care for each one as I would want my parents to be treated. They may tell me the same stories time after time but I don't mind. My regret is that I never knew them when they were healthy and active. They have led amazing lives. Their faith is something they teach me about constantly."

"I can imagine. So you aren't a pastor, an ordained clergy.

"No, I'm called a lay chaplain. I completed a course called Clinical Pastoral Education at the hospital here. I am a certified chaplain, but I am not ordained." she explained.

"Could you be a pastor if you wanted to?"

"If I went to the seminary for a few years, yes, but I'm too old now."

Glen straightened in his seat and leaned forward. "No, you are not too old. You are never too old for anything you want to do."

"Twenty years ago, it would have been different. Today, it would be a waste of time and money, especially mine. I could never get my investment back in the working years that I have left. I'd have to work until I'm eighty years old. I don't want to work that long. I have had enough learning, I want to use the training and talent I have now."

"Yes, I see what you mean," he nodded in agreement. He just leaned back and studied her face and said no more.

"What?" She asked feeling like he was seeing through her.

"Nothing, just looking." He was thinking, he liked what he saw.

She felt a flush. They were both silent a few moments. Taking a sip of her lemonade, Deb spoke. "What about you? It's been over thirty years. I heard you went out east, Washington, D. C."

"I taught in Marshall, Minnesota a few years and then got a job working for the government, so I moved to Washington. I was there for twenty-two years. It was interesting except for the noise, traffic and dirt. One kind of gets used to it, but we Midwesterners get lonesome for clean, uncluttered spaces."

"I heard you were married out there."

"From Mildred through Connie, I'm sure." They both nodded. "Yes, my wife's name was Myrna. She had been married before and had three kids when I met her. They were eight, ten, and eleven then, two boys and a girl. It was quite a package but we got along as well as can be expected. They were good kids."

"A ready-made family, and did you have more?" Deb asked.

"No." He stopped, looked down for a moment. "There were times when I would have liked to have my own ancestors but it seemed that three kids were enough to raise. Their dad was close by in Virginia so that helped. We thought it was important to stay near him so the kids could spend time with him."

"You're lucky it worked out so well. That isn't always the case."

"Well, there were some problems. It isn't easy for kids to live in two separate homes but we did the best we could. I tried not to make waves. That took away some of my power or authority."

Nodding in agreement, Deb said, "there are worse things than raising kids the way you did." *My own kids, I often wondered if their lives would have been better or worse, if I had separated completely from their father. Or was it better the way it was, just pretending he was there. I'd never know.* She didn't share it.

"You said you live in Minneapolis now."

"St. Paul, I work there. I live in a suburb. I moved back after Myra died."

"Oh, I'm sorry, I didn't realize." Deb started.

"You mean, you would have gone to coffee with me even if I was married? What is this? I can't believe it! Are you one of those women?" He acted shocked.

"For goodness sake," Deb laughed. "This is modern times." She turned as if she didn't want anyone else to hear. "We are in broad daylight, in public and already know each other. Of course I would and do especially if it's an old friend, why yes." She thought, *besides, sometimes a woman gets desperate for male conversation and company.*

Glen laughed too. "Old is right. There's no problem since we're both single. Now where was I? Oh, yes. The kids were grown and in college, on their own by then. One of them, Tami even lives in the Twin Cities. The other two, boys are still out east." He stopped. "Anyway, I've been back in St. Paul for over six years."

"Your wife died? What happened?" She was used to coming right out with it in her work. Asking a general question gives the person freedom to share whatever he or she wants, either go into detail or brush it off quickly. "If you want to tell me." Deb knew that most people want to talk but don't want to be pushed or feel like they are burdening another.

Glen looked in Deb's face wondering if he should, then took a deep breath before he started. "No, I don't mind talking about it. It was so many years ago and I haven't talked about it for a long time. We worked in the same building where I met Myrna. She was already divorced by then. She told me she'd had one bout with cancer several years before we met. She thought she had licked it. Then, when it came back, it came with a vengeance. This time it was in her bones, the spine."

"Oh no, bone cancer is very painful." Deb shared.

Glen twisted in his seat and turned his glass. "It was hell for her. The pain nearly drove her crazy. Nothing seemed to help. Euthanasia doesn't seem so wrong at times like that. It takes a strong, certain kind of faith to let God do it in His time."

"I know, you have to be really strong to not want to help the end come. We want our agenda, not God's." Deb agreed.

"Did that happen to you, someone in your life?" He asked.

"My dad," she shared, so he would know she understood. "It is hell for everyone, but also for those who can only watch and wait."

"Yes," he shifted in his seat again. "And not be able to do a thing to help. Just to be there and watch and wait. You wish they'd die and get it over with. She went from this attractive woman to a nearly bald skeleton, wreathing in pain or in a fog from the morphine." Glen stretched out and folded his hands on the table, playing with his fingers. "You don't want them to die but are relieved when it's over and they can be at peace." He clasped his hands, holding them tight.

Instinctively, Deb reached across the table and put her hand over his. He grabbed her fingers and held them tightly. When he looked up, he studied her face again. "You are good at this, you know."

"What?"

"I mean, you are good at your job. You do have a talent for pastoral care. I thought I was over it, it was so long ago. Myrna, the pain and death. Guess it's just been a long time since I've talked about it with anyone. The people I am close to, friends and associates in the cities never knew her so it never comes up. Sometimes, old memories come back. I try not to dwell on them but I think it is helpful to talk about it once in a while. It feels good now. You are so easy to talk to."

"I'm off duty now." Deb hoped to ease the tension. Then she squeezed his hands with hers. "I would rather be a friend you can talk to." She smiled and tried to pull her hand away.

"You're good at that too." He smiled back and released her hands after he squeezed them again. "You know how to ease the tension. Thanks." Glen cleared his throat and Deb knew he had said enough.

After a swallow of her drink, she waited a bit. "The kids,

Myrna's kids, are you still in touch with them?" A change of subject was in order.

"Yes, in fact sticking it out with Myrna and her illness made them appreciate me. I think they like me better now. Tami lives in the cities, and I see her and her family now and then. They share their two kids who call me Grandpa. I guess kids can't have too many grandparents."

"That's for sure. So, what do you do in St. Paul?"

"I'm in a construction business with a friend of mine. It's not a large company, so work is more relaxed. I like the slower pace. I had an apartment downtown and then found a townhouse on a lake north in St. Paul a couple of years ago."

"One of those 10,000 lakes in Minnesota?" She teased.

"Yes!" He said defensively.

"We call them sloughs in North Dakota." He laughed and nodded.

⚔ CHAPTER 5 ⚓

TWO HOURS HAD PASSED AND SO had several refills of lemonade and popcorn. "Glen, I need to find a restroom, the lemonade."

"Me too. Besides, lemonade and popcorn don't qualify for dinner. Do you feel like some real food? I do." They got up. He left some money on the table and they walked together to the restrooms.

"Later," was all Deb said pushing the door open on the Ladies Room. She thought while she was there, "*It sounds like he hasn't had enough of me.*"

Glen thought *he'd taken enough of Deb's time. She might even have other plans tonight. Maybe she has had enough of me by now. Here I am dominating her time.* Deb was nowhere when he came out so he waited.

When Deb came into the hallway, Glen was leaning against the wall. *Nice,* she thought, *it feels good. It's been a long time since I had a man wait for me or even wanted one to.*

He put his hand on her back as they stepped out the door of the coffee shop. "I started to ask you if you wanted to go somewhere else for dinner but didn't finish. Unless you have other plans this evening."

"Well, I had other plans, big ones. I was planning to go to the concert in the park. It's the last one and the music is bluegrass tonight. I was hoping to talk one of my granddaughters into going with me but hadn't gotten around to it." Deb shared. "Otherwise, I usually go alone. As you can see, I have a heavy social calendar. You could join me or we could skip it together." She offered. They were at Deb's car. "Well?" She turned to him.

Glen accepted. "I haven't gone to a concert in the park for years and I like bluegrass. How about getting some subs and a beverage and having a picnic?"

"Good idea." She agreed. "We have just enough time to make it. I'll drive since I know where to go. Ok?"

He got into the passenger seat with his long legs. Deb was glad she had a van with space. A quick stop at a deli shop and they had subs, chips, and soft drinks. She drove to Settler's Park and found a spot for the car. Glen grabbed the two lawn chairs from the back of the car, Deb took the food and they found an empty spot near the bandstand. They sat, dividing their meal.

Glen turned to Deb. "Would you like to pray?" Without waiting, he took her hand. "Lord, God, bless our food, fellowship and fun. Let our time together again be a blessing to us and to you, in Jesus' name, Amen."

Deb felt a stirring inside that was hard to shake off. Was it the prayer, the person or both? "Thank you."

The musicians were setting up already. Several people that

Deb knew came by but didn't stop to visit since the concert was beginning. They said hello and smiled a lot. Deb noticed eyebrows and stares during the concert. She forgot about people she knew seeing her with a man. Glen nudged her as one lady kept staring. He asked Deb if his lipstick was smeared. She poked him back, laughing.

When the band finished, they gathered up their belonging, placing them in the car as the park train came across the bridge blowing its whistle.

"Ever ride on the train?" Glen asked.

"Not for a long time." Deb admitted.

"Wanna ride tonight?"

"Sure, if we aren't too late."

"Let's hurry then." Glen grabbed her hand and started to walk fast. With a blast of the whistle, the train pulled into the station. His long stride increased as he pulled Deb along. "Come on!" He called over his shoulder.

"I can't run! They'll wait for us." Deb laughed.

"But, we've got a train to catch!"

"Yeah, I know, unless we miss it because I fall and break something."

He slowed down and took her arm. "Sorry."

Laughing and squealing, several families got onto the open scaled-down model train. The kids couldn't decide where to sit. Deb and Glen picked a bench near the back so they could watch it all. After everyone was seated, the conductor started up. "Last train for the night." He called. It began with a jerk and a sway, blowing its whistle at every crossing.

After a few minutes, Glen pointed. "The zoo! Does the

train go through the zoo?" He sounded like an excited kid. "How about the zoo, do you ever go?"

"I haven't been there this year. I have a grandparent's membership so can take grandchildren free. I take my grand kids when they come. I could take you but you probably wouldn't qualify for admission on my pass." Deb joked.

"Gosh!" Glen remarked. "I remember when that building right over there was the monkey house. Boy, did it stink in there. We had to go in though to watch those silly monkeys."

"They're outside now over there." Deb pointed to a caged area. You wouldn't recognize the old monkey house today. It's a gift shop and information center; a place where kids can do crafts and learn about the animals. There are all kinds of hands-on displays the kids can touch, tables and chairs, almost a library. And it doesn't stink!"

The train swerved and swayed around a sharp curve, throwing Deb against Glen. His arm was across the back of the seat, so he just grabbed her by the shoulder to hold her up. Then he pulled her closer to him. It felt good and they smiled at each other. "Opportunities corner!" He said softly near her ear. Glen was aware of her touch from then on as the train jerked and swayed. Neither moved away from each other.

The train pulled up to the platform. "All out!" The conductor shouted blowing the whistle. Just like the kids on the train, Deb wanted it to last longer. They walked slowly to the car. She drove back to the hotel and pulled under the portico.

"Glen..." Deb turned toward him. "I'm so glad you called me. It's been fun to see you."

" I haven't done my business yet. I have to see a lawyer tomorrow. I took a couple of days off so I'm in no hurry. Deb, could I see you again before I go? I'd like to." Glen spoke softly.

"Me too. Yes, I'd like that too." Deb tried not to seem too eager.

He touched her cheek, turning her face toward him leaning forward, he brushed his lips across hers. Surely he could hear her heart beat, Deb could. Close to her face he said "I have to let you go." Deb just sat there. Glen opened the door and was gone. She wondered if she should be driving when her arms and legs felt so weak.

What is the problem here? The difference between Glen and those other guys is, I was usually glad the evening was over and I was home. I didn't want this one to end and could hardly wait for tomorrow when I would see Glen again.

She didn't know how she got home. She just remembered driving into the quonset and shutting the door. Walking across the yard on rubber legs, she opened the screen, unlocked the door and hurried to get into bed to relax her legs. She just dropped her clothes in a pile on the floor and slid between the sheets.

Now was the time for a good scolding. *After my marriage to Dan, and now that's over, I'm finally alone which I love. My job and living here in this place, all of it that I love. How can I even think of getting serious about a man? I resolved five years ago, no men, no* man. *A date to an event, a meal with some man who wants to cry on my shoulder. Sometimes, it was almost unbearable.*

I have resolved for over two years, that I need nothing else. I love my freedom, my aloneness, doing my own thing, no man to work around or take care of.

Now, I get this dopy feeling like weakness in the knees, flutters in my chest. He just wants to have fun while he is here. He will go back to the city and his life. We can just have fun and enjoy it while we can and let it all go in a day or two. Deb rationalized as she lay there.

✧ CHAPTER 6 ✧

GLEN WALKED TO THE ELEVATOR FEELING unsteady. He wondered *what's gotten into me? The fact that I made a move at all amazed me. I didn't want to scare her off. It just seemed right to kiss her. It wasn't a passionate kiss, but I got the feeling she liked it.* As he got on the elevator, he realized he hadn't made a real plan or set a time with her. *That's what happens when a guy hasn't dated for years. I'm out of practice. What a jerk! I guess I surprised myself too, when I kissed her and then I just needed to get away. Now I need to call her back.*

He reached for the phone. *What am I doing? Stop it! Well, it's just a date, just going out for dinner or whatever with a woman.* He dialed Deb's number. It rang.

"Hello, Glen?"

"How did you know it was me?"Glen asked.

"Well, the last time the phone rang it was you so it had to be you this time. Guess I just know your ring."

"Are you psychic?"

"No, I'm Deb" she joked.

"I feel like George Burns talking to Gracie Allen. Now I can't remember who I am or why I called." Laughing, he

30

continued. "Oh, yeah. I asked you if I could see you again and then didn't make plans before you left. Guess I was too shook."

"Shook?" Deb repeated.

"Yeah, shook," he said again laughing through his teeth.

"That word dates you, sir. I haven't heard it for a long time."

"Yes, well, it's been a long time since I was shook or asked a woman for a date or even wanted to." He confessed. "It's a sad story."

"I'd like to hear it sometime." Then she shared her feelings. "As I drove off, I had this old feeling like when I was a teenager and a guy said he'd call. I knew I would never hear from him again. It is also a sad story."

"We have a lot of sad stuff, huh? Did you think I was one of those guys?" He sounded sincere.

"Not really, but I admit it bothered me more that I'd regressed to my insecure youth for a few minutes." She admitted.

"Are you okay now that the guy called?" He teased.

"Yes, thanks, I feel better. Except that, I probably would have called you now but certainly wouldn't have forty years ago. You gave me your number, you know. So, how about that date?"

"You are direct. Ahem," he cleared his throat. "Yes, Ms. Sullivan, would you accompany me on a dinner date tomorrow?"

"Yes, Mr. Jarvis, I'd like that. Now, you said you had to see your lawyer.

"Oh, that's in the morning." He said.

"In the morning I have yard work to do early and hospital people to see later. So, let me tell you how to get to my house so you may come whenever you are ready." She gave him directions to her house and then said "I should be home by four or five. Actually, you could come in the morning and help me with my yard work."

"Ah, can't. I didn't bring gardening clothes." He grinned.

"Excuses, excuses. Well, how about dinner at six or six thirty."

"Great. See you tomorrow. Good night, Deb."

"Good night, Glen and Glen?"

"Yes?"

"Thank you for today. I'm glad you called me."

"Me too. G'night."

"G'night." Deb lay back on the pillow hanging up the phone. *"Oh, I need to call Eileen back or she won't sleep tonight worrying about me."* She picked up the phone again and pushed her memory number.

"Hello?" Eileen sounded excited.

"It's me, Deb." She said. "Thought I had better call you before you have a stroke."

"Well, one never knows if you were with a mass murderer or rapist."

"Eileen, only you would think of that. It wasn't that exciting. Yes, I just got home. We talked all afternoon, went to the concert and rode the train in the park. How's that?"

"The train? How romantic!" Eileen cooed. "Did you like him? You have to tell me all about him."

"I think I told you one time, years ago. He's the guy

who wanted to call me for a date and then found out I was married."

"That one? Oh, for heaven sake! Well, you have to tell me the details again."

"Later though, I have to work part of the day and then we have a date for dinner." Deb bragged.

Eileen declared, "You have never gone out with a guy twice, this has to be something. Is he good looking, is this the tall one?"

"Yes, he is." Deb answered. "Oh, Eileen, he is so nice and we had such a good time. I can hardly wait to see him tomorrow."

"Well, you had better get your beauty sleep. I'll talk to you whenever, huh?"

"Call you later, bye." They hung up.

Eileen became Deb's first friend when she moved to Grand Island twenty years or so ago. They had a lot in common, controlling husbands, and rotten marriages. They had a pact that they wouldn't say something bad about their husbands unless they said something good right afterward. So they quit talking about them all together. Deb didn't know what she would have done without Eileen's support all of these years.

Glen stripped to his shorts and crawled between the sheets. He looked at the clock. It's only 10:00. *What am I doing? What's to come of this? Why am I worried about it? We did click. At the very least, it would be fun to have a female friend to do things with and go places with. Would "friends" kiss on the first date? Well, she let me and she's going to see me again, so. It seemed like the right thing to do and I'm glad I did,* he reassured himself before sleep set in.

When Glen woke in the morning, he remembered tossing and turning during the night. Deb seemed to be there in his dream. Thinking of yesterday and Deb, *I'm so grateful I called her. From the moment I saw her coming across the parking lot, I had the feeling we would click. Yesterday, I wondered what would come of this. Today, I look forward to seeing her again.* He showered, shaved, and dressed. He'd slept in but still had plenty of time before going to the lawyer's office. He kept thinking of Deb so he took the directions he'd written down and his briefcase and decided to see if he could find Deb's place.

⚔ CHAPTER 7 ⚔

DEB WOKE AT 5:30 AM, A lifetime habit. *Some mornings, I doze for a while. Other times it is special to just lay here in my bed, thinking of how pleasant life is, just the peace and privacy. I no longer had to answer to anyone. I love living alone, being on my own, but not lonely. After forty years of marriage when I was alone more of the time than not and yearning for companionship and affection. Now, I'm alone by choice and I like it. In fact, I savor it, feeling resentment when my solitude is broken. When the phone rings, I dread who will interrupt my privacy.*

Thirty years as a full-time mother of four, five if I include Dan, I was always "on call". Often, I was the mother and father. I did take my motherhood job seriously, trying to be the kind of mother I thought my kids needed. The empty nest syndrome never bothered me. I was glad when the kids became adults and were on their own. It gave me the opportunity to look around and do something with the rest of my life. I found it fun and exciting.

Four years ago, I moved here to Grand Island. Dan chose to stay in Mallory for another two years or so. "Then, he promised, he'd retire and move here with me." He had several offers of positions here in Grand Island. I felt hurt that he would sacrifice our marriage for his love of money, and power, being a big fish in a little pond. By then I had no expectations of him. It was just the final blow, the end of any hope that our marriage would work. It was time to quit trying to keep this leaky boat afloat. There were too many holes to plug and I was the only one working at it. I really didn't like boating all that much!

Oh, I hate it when I start thinking about it all again. It's all so negative and depressing. There is no reason for it today especially. Today there is Glen Jarvis. I couldn't ignore the feeling deep inside that struck a few times when I was with him. When he searched my face as we sat talking in the restaurant, I felt like he saw the "real" Debra Sullivan. Then he surprised me by taking my hand to pray before we ate, it seemed so natural and touched me like he always did that. I liked the feeling when he held me around the corner on the train ride and then just held me. I was surprised he kissed me as he got out of the car. Gosh, I hardly know him, what is the matter with me. I knew him years ago, didn't I? Not really.

Where would he fit in my life? Don't jump the gun, girl. He's just a date, and an enjoyable time. We'll have this date and he will go back to the big city and we'll resume our former lives. I knew I hoped differently.

Ah, "this truly is the day the Lord has made". She paraphrased the Psalm verse and "I will rejoice and be glad in it".

She felt good, loved this room, pale green, soft pink with white and creamy lace that made the room soft and feminine. The bedroom set was Deb's one extravagance when she moved here. The queen-sized bed was high and soft, surrounded by a bedroom wall of mirrored shelves and a bookcase. It was Deb.

Today she has a date! She got up, straightened her room, and slipped on shorts, tennis shoes, and a long-sleeved shirt. She swallowed her meds with a glass of water, then downed a glass of juice and went out to the quonset. She had mowing to do. First she checked the oil, then filled the gas tank on her trusty John Deere 320 and climbed aboard. It started on the first try and she was off.

She mowed around the huge evergreens west of the house. There were thirty-seven of them in the yard. They had grown between twenty and thirty feet tall. They could be mean, scratching one's arms and legs if you mowed too close. But Deb loved them. It was dusty from lack of rain so she was getting dirty. She only had two strips left on the east side of the house, when a blue pickup roared down the driveway. She knew it was Glen even though she couldn't see the driver. Deb waved and turned around for the final strip.

Coming back toward the driveway, Glen was leaning against his truck. That stirring feeling came back to her gut so she quickly chose to ignore it. He smiled and waved as Deb lifted her mower blade, turned off the PTO and drove past him toward the quonset. By the time she parked, Glen had followed her inside. He had a grin on his face like he enjoyed watching the whole scene.

"Good morning," he smiled.

"Good morning, you found me." Deb said. He still had that smile or was it a grin? "What?" She asked as she got off the tractor feeling a little shaky walking. Was it from two hours on the mower? "What, you love work, you could watch it all day?"

"You." He smiled. "You seem to enjoy your work. You were raised on a farm so it is natural, right?."

"Yes, as a matter of fact, I was the farmer's daughter. How did you know?" She asked as they walked to the house.

"You told me one time."

"I did?"

"Uh huh, one time in an intimate conversation." He teased

"Oh? That's intimate." She threw back at him.

"You mow like a pro and your yard looks like it too." He complimented her.

"It's really dry now but thank you. I do enjoy it. I never rode the tractor until the kids left home. Say, you're a bit early for our date, what are you doing here now? Did you decide to help after all?" She teased.

"Just came to see if I could follow your directions. I had a little time and a lot of curiosity." He confessed. "You told me you had a beautiful place, so I came to see for myself. You were right." They went up on the deck and leaned against the railing. He looked out over the ravine. Turning to her, "did I interrupt you, stop you from your work?"

"No, I would have quit when I did. I don't do it all at once."

"How many acres do you have? How long does it take?"

"Well, I have 5 acres but I don't mow it all. Some is pasture. I mow about three acres in about six hours. Then there is trimming to do."

"Now I see what you love here, not just the scenery but the privacy."

"In the fall like this, it's especially beautiful." She added.

"How long have you owned this place?" Glen asked.

"Oh, over twenty years. We bought it when we first moved here from Mallory. Then it never sold when we moved back so we leased it. When I decided to come back, I had a place to go. I planned to sell it then. It was too much to keep up. In fact I had a buyer and Dan talked me out of it. He thought we needed a place like this. Space to spread out in." *I didn't need to add what I was thinking, that we needed enough space to avoid each other.*

They stood there without saying anything. The birds, the wind- in-the-trees. Traffic on the highway off in the distance was the only sound.

"Do you see wild animals here?" He asked as he looked around.

"Yes, the usual rabbits, gophers, squirrels..."

"I was thinking more of.."

"Deer." They said it together.

"Deer, yes, they come right into the yard close to the house. There is a flock of wild turkeys and some pheasants around. I've even seen owls and Golden and American eagles."

"Really?" He looked at her.

"Lotta wild life, besides the animals." She joked, trying to relax his stare. Now she felt sort of lightheaded, like she was going to fall over. "I need a drink. How about you?" He was too close and they looked at each other too long. Deb turned away toward the sliding door. She could breathe again. "Come on in." He followed. "Have a chair. What will you have?"

"Whatever you have." He sat at the table looking around."Country Kitchen, well done."

She poured juice and sat across from him. "I had it

redone when we moved here. Well, I need to take a shower. Make yourself comfortable. Look around. Pick some weeds, whatever." She said the last words over her shoulder as she left the room.

"You never give up." He shook his head, then finished his juice and set their glasses in the sink. Then he walked around the house and across the yard. He took the morning paper from its tube and walked to the top of the road. He turned back to the house and surveyed the view. The neighbor was trimming some bushes by his door. They waved to each other but didn't speak. Huge evergreens stood in stately rows framing two sides of the property. No wonder Deb loves it here.

He stopped on the sidewalk in front of the flowerbed. Deb had well-trimmed bushes mixed with annuals and perennials. She must be a rock hound. There were rocks of every shape, size, and color piled and laid out to look natural around the plants. He liked it.

Deb came out the front door. "There you are. Picking a few weeds?"

"Couldn't find any," he said as she stopped beside him.

"You really do need your eyes examined."

"Ya know what? I'm hungry after all my farm chores. I'll buy breakfast if you'll drive or do you have time?"

Checking his watch, he said, "just barely," Glen took Deb's arm and steered her to his truck. He opened the door, waited for her to get in, and shut it. He smiled through the window, then went to his side. That funny feeling inside of her hit whenever he was that close. She was sure he could tell. He climbed into the cab. He had plenty of room for his long legs in this vehicle.

Deb directed him to her favorite breakfast place close by, Cathy's Café. Seated in a booth, they pored over the menu, ordered, and ate, then sipped their coffee. Suddenly, Glen looked at his watch. "I need to see my lawyer in fifteen minutes."

"And I have to go to work." He dropped her at her house and roared up the hill. Deb had to leave too. Today, she had hospitalized members to care for.

✠ CHAPTER 8 ✠

DEB LIKED HOSPITAL CALLS. PATIENTS WERE a captive audience, too sick or weak to leave and not strong enough to kick her out. They usually appreciated visitors if one didn't stay too long.

One of her favorite older men, Simon Vermeer was getting better after a serious operation. Pneumonia set in the second day as it often did with elderly. He was out of the ICU now but still pretty weak.

It hurt to see the torture families put their parents through just to keep them alive a few more months or perhaps a year. Pneumonia used to be a friend to the elderly. They would just go to sleep and be gone. Now, they had to be cured, sometimes more than once.

Today Simon smiled in contrast to the helpless figure he was a few days ago when his eyes seemed to beg for help. Deb visited with him about his progress. She changed the subject when he started to talk about going home. He was probably destined for a nursing home. The social workers would evaluate him and his care soon. Deb shared Simon's favorite,

Psalm100 and a prayer with him. She promised to be back in a few days. He said he'd be home by then. She answered, "I pray so."

The next visit was a woman named, Mary Winthrup. She was about fifty years old. She had a severe stroke that impaired her speech. She could only slur several words. Her future looked bleak unless rehab restored her ability to communicate. Now she seemed to have given up. It was hard to offer her hope unless her attitude changed. Her daughter said the doctor was giving her antidepressants to see if she would be more cooperative with the rehab staff. Deb talked with her about her therapy and prayed with her for recovery so she could live her life as before.

Then she visited Norma who had surgery the day before. Her entire family was crowded into her room. She'd made it through the surgery and was sleeping. With Deb's hand on her shoulder and everyone in a circle around her bed, they shared a prayer for her recovery and her family's support and patience. Her condition was fragile but if family support helped, she should make it.

Her last hospital call was a diabetic man named Fred Taylor. He had an ulcerated sore on his foot. He was one of her shut-ins she had known for several years. She sat by his bed to visit awhile. He said his sore was healing and he would go home tomorrow. He was more concerned about his wife, Rosie than himself. "She worries too much and wears herself out taking care of me." Though she didn't seem to have any major health problems, Rosie was after all eighty-two years old.

He asked Deb to come and visit his wife after he got home. Perhaps over a cup of coffee Deb could convince Rosie to get help to take care of him. But he said not to tell her. Deb promised. She told him how impressed she was with his concern for his wife, Rosie. Deb thought their marriage was really special. They cared so much for each other after all of these years. She told him so. He said they'd been married almost sixty-five years now and he loves Rosie now as much as he ever did. Fred got tears in his eyes as he spoke of her. "She is so precious to me... and I think she loves me too." He whispered the last part.

Deb whispered back. "I think you're right. I envy what you have. Most couples never share love like you two have. You are truly blessed."

"You should have it too. Everyone should experience this kind of marriage," Fred said. "Aren't you married?"

"I was. My husband died some time ago. I don't think we ever had what you two have."

"Well, you still can, you can try again. You're young enough to have another love. You shouldn't be alone for the rest of your life. You have lots of good years left. Man was not meant to be alone, nor was woman. It's biblical, you know." He preached the last sentences.

"Perhaps, but I rather like living alone. I was a wife for forty years and a full-time mother of four kids for over thirty years. Being alone now feels good. I'm alone but not lonely most of the time. I doubt that I can find someone I'd want to give that up for."

He winked at her. "If you do, grab him and hang on." Deb smiled back at him. They shared a prayer and she gave him some reading material. She gave Fred a hug goodbye. He grinned from ear to ear.

What Fred said rang in Deb's ears. Strange she would have this conversation today. Was Fred her messenger? Did it take a Fred for her to at least be open to whatever life might hold? A relationship with a man was debatable. Deb didn't tell Fred about Glen.

Glen found his lawyer's office downtown. They visited for a while and then signed the papers, making the sale of the last of the Jarvis Family Farm legal. Now it's gone. He placed his copies in his briefcase and left. As he drove away, he had a sense of loss. It was like the grief he felt when his parents died, when Chris was killed in the car crash and when Myrna died too. This was just land, family farmland, true, but land all the same. It was gone now, no longer part of their family. Glen had paid Chris's boys their father's total share when he sold part of the farm ten years ago after Chris died. Glen thought the boy and their mom needed the money then, rather than wait until Glen died and left it to them.

Glen's grandparents had homesteaded the farm back in the early 1900s. Grandpa Jarvis loved farming. So did Glen's Dad, Henry. Henry lived on the homestead all of his life. When he married, he moved his wife, Olive there. It was their home until he retired.

Neither Chris nor Glen wanted to farm. Their parents had to be disappointed but never told them that. They wanted the boys to have a college education so when they got one, they pursued other occupations. Glen knew he was lucky that his parents had wanted most for him to be happy.

Now they were all gone, the whole family and now the whole farm is gone. There's no getting any of it back now, the people or the property. He felt sad and alone.

Glen at least had his dinner date to look forward to. He still had too much time before he dared go to Deb's again so he went to the mall. It had grown a lot since he had seen it last. Glen just walked, until he saw a gift shop. He went in and picked out a vase he liked. He had several roses arranged in the vase and had it gift-wrapped.

It was still too early to go to Deb's so he decided to drive by the farmstead where he grew up. *Who knows if I will ever come back here?* He thought. It was seventeen miles north, then half a mile west of Grand Island. Even after all of these years, it just seemed automatic to turn onto County Road #28W. He didn't even have to think about it. Two miles ahead, he slowed, turned off the gravel road and pulled into the approach to the farmstead. The house was gone. It had been moved off years ago. The basement foundation was a crumbling mass of stone and mortar with weeds tangled around it. Just the granary that leaned south from all of the years of north-west winds. A pile of boards and shingles was all that was left of the magnificent structure that once was the barn. Rusted machinery stuck out of the tall grass beyond the trees. The shelter belt had once protected the yard from winter blasts and shaded the house from the hot afternoon sun. The trees had passed their life span now. Most of them were rotted and hollow, falling against each other. Few leaves remained on their broken branches. Like skeletons of the past, they no longer were attractive or protective.

Glen didn't get out of the truck. He just sat there. *I wish Chris was here to share this with me. I miss my older brother. His death had been so sudden at forty-eight, too young. He died in a crash coming back from a coach's meeting in Minneapolis. I feel robbed of the years we could have had together. Now I need someone to reminisce with, share it. He should be here.*

He swung his pickup around in the approach and headed back down the road. He waited for a grain truck to pass. The driver waved the usual Midwestern greeting. Glen waved back but didn't feel very friendly. He pulled onto the highway as he had done so many times in his life. He realized his mind was only half on his driving.

⤃ CHAPTER 9 ⤃

GLEN LOOKED AROUND. NOW HE KNEW where he was driving over the hill into Deb's yard. He needed someone to talk to, to share with, like coming home. He yearned for "home" but Deb's? What made him come here?

He rang the doorbell. The inside door was open. Through the screen door, Deb called, "Come on in." Glen stepped inside and her voice came from the bedroom area. "You're early. I'll be right there." He started to sit down when Deb came down the hall so he stood back up.

Deb heard Glen's truck and soon the doorbell rang. He was an hour early. She called for him to come in. Lucky she had gotten ready early. Smearing on some lipstick and checking the mirror, Deb came down the hallway. Glen was standing in front of the sofa. He had a look on his face that she couldn't read but it was different. She motioned for him to sit down. In one stride he swept her into his arms and murmured, "I need a… hug." He seemed tense or stiff. At first, Deb reached her arms around his waist and hugged him back with her head on his chest. He still held her tight.

"What, Glen? What's happened?" He released her and she led him to the sofa to sit. She held his hand trying to read his face. Why was he acting this way? "Glen, what happened to you? Did something go wrong?" She took both of his hands.

"Well, not wrong exactly." He shook his head as if to clear his thoughts. "I'm sorry, Deb. I don't know why I came here like this, to your house. I hope you don't mind. I just need to talk to someone and you are the best someone I know here, anywhere. It was more emotional than I thought it would be, selling the farm."

"What, selling your land?" Deb guessed. "I didn't know that was what your business was. I'm sorry."

"Yes, it was the last of our, my families farmland. And then I drove out to the farm, the old farmstead. I didn't realize it would be such an emotional thing. There was a feeling of loss when I left the lawyer's office. That was enough. Then I drove to the farm and added to it. I missed Chris, wished he were here to share it with me. Then I missed Mom and Dad and everyone. I felt so… alone."

"In terms of immediate family, you are alone. They aren't here to share this with you. You returned to the grief you felt when they first died. It comes around again when something like this triggers it. You are the last one in your family to carry these memories for all of you. I would expect it to be emotional for you, for anyone.

You have Chris' boys to share those memories with if you want to. Have they been to the farm? Were they young enough when Chris died that he hadn't told them about their past, their heritage?"

"I don't know," he mused. "Yeah, they probably had been

there when my folks were still on the farm. I'll have to find out one day but for now..." He went silent. So did Deb.

"Glen, it's understandable that you would feel loss and grief. We have feelings for things and places too. They hold memories, good and bad. They are yours."

"I had the same feelings when my folks and Chris and Myrna died. But this is just land, actually a sheet of paper. Why would a person feel that way about a thing like land?"

Deb squeezed his hand. He pulled it to his face so she touched him there. "Glen, it isn't just a piece of paper, the land, the farm, the dirt that you grieve over. It is your life, memories, feelings about that place. It is much more than dirt or land that you mourn. There is your family and all of those memories. It's a lot to take in at once."

He put his arm around her shoulder. He pulled her closer. "Glen, tell me about the farm. Describe it, what you remember about it."

He took a deep breath, kept his arm around her shoulder. "I drove out there and it really hurt. The house was sold and moved off years ago. I knew that but I had a picture of it in my mind. There's just a bit of foundation showing now. It was one of those big farmhouses, ya know, three stories, always painted white. It had a big front porch with a swing hanging from the roof. The porch was home base whenever we played games. Yeah, home base." He smiled and so did Deb. "It had a big farm kitchen with a large round oak table in the middle, you know." She nodded. "That was where we played games and did our homework. Company always ended up there, talking and drinking coffee. It always smelled good in there. Mom was a good cook. She couldn't make enough cookies to fill us up.

We could hardly wait to get home for cookies and milk and run and play after sitting in school all day. "We brought friends home to play a lot. Riding the school bus was boring and a waste of time but our friends liked to ride the bus and come to play at the farm. We'd climb into the hayloft in the barn and play in the hay. It was itchy but fun. Dad always had cows. I liked the smell of the barn, the fresh hay and wood smells. I loved that smell. I can still imagine it. I thought it was a grand building then." He stopped. Deb could feel him stiffen. "Now, it has fallen to one side in a pile of weathered wood. There's an old granary bent away from the wind. Sad." He finished.

He was quiet for a while. Then shifting on the sofa and adjusting himself next to Deb while holding her close with his grip on her shoulder. Glen didn't realize how physically close they were or maybe he did. The feeling deep inside her was almost painful. He brushed his lips on her forehead. She could feel his breath through her hair. The feeling down inside her seemed to radiate into her limbs. It was hard to concentrate on what he was saying. She just sat still not wanting to break the spell.

"The shelter belts, those rows of trees surrounding the farmstead. I guess we took for granted that it would always be there. We used to run in and out of them, playing bandits and cowboys. Kids didn't have space people to fight then but it was the same kind of play. You could really hide in the trees and tall grass. There were lots of places to hide on the farm. We climbed most of those trees. Some of them were apple trees and from the time I think I was six, it was our job to climb the apple trees or get out the ladders to get the apples at the top. We weren't supposed to bruise them. But we picked them all." He stopped, thinking. "The trees are all dead and falling over now."

Now he grinned. "We had the run of the place, all the space we needed. We didn't just play either. We had chores to do on the farm. We helped feed and water the animals summer and winter. Cleaning the barn wasn't fun but we did it. Kids don't have that any more."

"I know." Deb pulled away and looked in his face. "What you feel are memories, stories to tell and share if you want to. Glen, you can sell the land, have the buildings hauled away and the rest of the place may be run down, but no one can take away the memories you have. The fun and joy and even the tragedy and pain you might have had there, no one can rob you of that. In fact, that will always be yours, alone. You could share it though."

He turned to her. "Deb, I came here to you like I was coming home for comfort. I laid this on you because I felt like I could and it would be safe with you. I guess this is the closest to a home I have now. I knew you would listen and care."

"I wish I would have gone to the farm with you."

"Me too." He agreed.

"I would have made you tell me stories and point to the very places where they happened."

"You would have made it adventurous instead of sad." Glen looked at her and she saw a tenderness that made her melt. The feeling in her gut, that almost-pain was there again. "Thank you, Deb. Now I know why I came here. I was sent to you."

"You could have shared your story with anyone." She brushed it off.

"I didn't want to share it with anyone, I needed to share it with you. You helped the negative turn positive. The hurt that was there, you soothed it like rubbing a sore muscle. Then there is the other side of it."

"Other side?" Deb repeated.

"I don't have kids, issue of my own to share it with, children to tell the stories to so I guess it doesn't matter. My step children wouldn't understand. They were always city people. They probably don't even know what a farm looks like."

"You might be surprised how much they would enjoy stories of the farm they could never have experienced. Maybe that makes your story more important to tell. The same goes for your nephews and their families. Especially since their dad can't. You need to write it, share with them a gift from their dad's family."

"I'm not a writer," he confessed.

"Everyone is. You don't have to be to tell stories about your life. I could get you started. Once you do, you'll like it." Deb blurted out without realizing what that would mean. "I've helped lots of people get started. When you start to tell them stories about you and your brother's childhood, you'll think of more to tell."

Glen looked at Deb as if she said some magic words. "Would you help me?"

Now, she was in a bind. "If, well if there is a way I can, sure." He seemed to relax.

It dawned on her, "Was I being the counselor again?" .

"Yes, but no, not at all. You were being a caring friend. If it wasn't for you, I would not have come to Grand Island. I would have signed my papers and settled the farm sale by mail. Then I might have felt bad and never have known what hit me. I would have missed all of this. No, it was supposed to be this way, special."

"Maybe," Deb smiled. "Actually, I don't believe in chance or coincidence. I believe things happen when and how they are supposed to."

Glen leaned back, more relaxed now. For the first time since they sat down, he took his grip off her shoulder. He turned and looked at Deb and smiled. "God," was all he said as if a prayer. Then he took her hand. "You know what?"

"What?" Deb was afraid to ask.

⚔ CHAPTER 10 ⚕

"I'M HUNGRY, HOW ABOUT YOU?"

Deb nodded. "Starved! Let's go eat." He started to get up and turned to help her.

"I forgot something." He hurried out the door and came back with a gift for her. She opened it to find a dainty glazed translucent milk glass vase with three yellow roses in it.

"Oh, it's beautiful and milk glass. Thank you. How did you know?" He smiled and pointed to the china closet with the other milk glass pieces. "You're so thoughtful. Thank you." Deb set the vase on the table, took a whiff of the roses and turned to Glen. She took his face in her hands softly and slowly kissed him. That feeling in her gut, it was there again. Glen just stood still, looking in her eyes. She stepped away from him. Without a word, they turned and left for dinner.

As he got into his truck, he turned to her. "You look gorgeous in your green outfit. Also, Deb, thank you for being here for me today. It seemed so right for me. I hope you don't think I need a counselor but a friend. I, you, ah could." then he stopped."Never mind." He started the truck and drove off. Deb wondered what he was going to say.

Talk about Grand Island, how it had grown and changed since Glen had last been there carried the conversation until they reach the El Rancho Supper Club. The club had good food as well as a quiet relaxed atmosphere. They ordered a drink and Glen started to read the vast menu.

"What's good? Or would you like me to just order a large steak for each of us since you're my date?" He smiled with his head down, looking at Deb through the top of his eyes.

"You, you remember that time, the time at the Elks?" Deb was amazed.

"Sure, how could I forget? I had a crush on you by the time that evening was over."

"But that was over thirty years ago! I never thought you would remember an incident so long ago. Glen, I'm sorry about that. I never dreamed you thought I was single."

Glen explained, "It wasn't anything you did. It was I who misunderstood, It was just wishful thinking on my part. Why should you feel badly?"

"I was flattered that you or anyone wanted to date me, but I felt badly that you were embarrassed by it. I hoped I hadn't led you on in any way."

"Well, you did." He cast his eyes down again. "You need to be more careful about how you toy with a man's feelings" he teased.

Deb laughed. "Really, I am sorry. Say you forgive me or I shall not be able to eat a bite of my huge steak."

"After a remark like that, I question your sincerity but ok, I forgive you."

"Thank you. What a relief!" They laughed.

"Honestly," Glen said. "I never forgot it though I wanted to. I really thought you were neat that night at the Elks. Then when I offered you a ride and you turned me down, I was sure you were just shy. I thought of you all the way back to Mallory. When I called Mildred to find out your phone number, I was shocked when she said you were married. Think if I would have just called you without knowing. I vowed to be more careful around you after that. I would ignore you, just stay away."

Deb answered, "Well, at least if you'd have called me directly, you wouldn't have had Mildred telling everyone in town about it. She could hardly wait to tell me how cute it was that you wanted to date me. Until we all were on our way to Fargo, I didn't realize everyone else knew too."

They ordered dinner and their reminiscing continued.

Glen began, "Did it embarrass you, personally, I mean?"

"No. Actually, I was flattered. I was convinced that I didn't have much attraction to anyone except maybe Dan and I didn't understand what he saw in me."

"You really don't know how attractive you are, do you?" He shook his head.

Embarrassed, she said "No, I never considered myself appealing in any way."

He shook his head again. "We will discuss that another time, Young Lady! What I meant was, did it concern you that folks in town might talk about you having males attracted to you, especially me?"

"No, first of all I had no such thoughts that I was attractive but there were always rumors about us from the time we moved to Mallory. Dan would not have had time to have all of the affairs the grapevine claimed. Though I believe there were some that were true. People never told me, they just gossiped together. I had to ignore the rumors or be destroyed. If there were stories about me, I never heard them, so I assumed there were none. I learned early to do my own thing and not be concerned with what others made of it. Dan was on his pedestal and I was to be his adoring helpmate. That was all that was expected of me. They preferred to talk about him."

Changing the topic somewhat, Glen studied Deb's face for a moment, then went on. "Did you know I was going to Fargo, to Mark's wedding?"

"Yes, and you knew I was going."

"Yes, but I found out by accident at Stag Night at the Country Club. When we came in from our round of golf, some of the guys were playing cards and Mark's Dad started giving Doctor Sullivan a bad time about not going to Mark's wedding. The doctor explained that he always went fishing that time of year. They said 'but everyone was going and we were spending the weekend there.' He argued that he couldn't go to both so he would go fishing. Then, they told him that I was going too, just about the time I came up to their table.

"Aren't you, Glen?" They turned to me. It seemed like they were teasing him so I got into it. 'Yes, I plan to go.'" I said. He seemed unshaken.

He just said 'hope you all have as good time. My wife will represent our family just fine.' Then he turned back to his card game.

The guys wouldn't let it die. They went on that you would be alone without a man and I was single and would be alone.

He said he trusted his wife. Then they reminded him that I had already shared a steak dinner with you a few months ago and how well we got along. Still, he continued to insist that he had every faith in his wife that she would remember she was married. He trusted her/you completely.

I should have left it at that but I would not have been so sure if I were the husband so I added 'you may trust her but can you trust me?' "

Doctor Sullivan just grinned. 'That's your problem.'"

This was the first Deb had heard the story that way. Her feelings of hurt and shame, that happened too many years ago came flooding back. She didn't want Glen to know how she still could feel the pain. Then Glen asked "Did Dr. Sullivan tell you about what happened at the Country Club?"

"Yes, she admitted. "But his version was brief. That was typical of Dan. He was a man of few words especially if it might be intimate or personnel. He just said 'The guys gave me a bad time last night about my not going to Mark's wedding. Glen Jarvis was there with Chris. They said he was going and insinuated that it might be a problem with the two of you there.'

I asked him what he said. He just said he told them that he trusted his wife completely. That's how I found out you were going to Fargo. The other guys told longer versions to their wives so I got several stories that filled in the gaps."

Glen searched her face. "How did you feel about that?"

"I was hurt." Her voice was soft as she choked up so she sipped her drink.

"Hurt?"

"Strange maybe but I needed Dan to say he was jealous, just a little. I wanted him to care enough to be jealous once." She was close to crying.

"I can understand that," Glen said.

"Can you really?" She was surprised. He nodded. "I don't sound childish, silly?"

"No, not to me."

"I wanted him to think I was alluring enough to attract another man. He put all of the responsibility on me to behave. It became my burden. Another means of controlling me, anything. That was Dan!" She was getting into her old resentments, so she tried to be flip about it.

"I understand Deb and I agree with you. If they had been giving me a bad time like that about my wife, I might have put on a front then but gone home and been affectionate to my wife just for reassurance.

I got the feeling he was controlling even there at the Country Club. Everyone seemed to know the conversation was over when he made his final statement. I felt uneasy that it started in a jovial note and ended abruptly. No jokes!"

"Yeah, but in the end, he went fishing and I went to the wedding weekend. That was life with Dan."

"You know, a lot of women would have stayed home without their controlling husband."

"I would have missed out on a lot of life if I had stayed home every time Dan couldn't or wouldn't go." She stopped, took a swallow of her drink. "Let's not talk about him now."

"I'm sorry, you're right. I guess it doesn't pay except I'm

glad I know your feelings." He raised his hand. "Say no more, deal?" He asked.

"Deal!" She declared in relief.

A second cocktail came and they ordered dinner. Salads and bread were served but the reminiscing continued.

"Is it ok if we talk about 'that weekend' as long as the doctor isn't part of it?" Glen asked, studying her reaction.

"Yes, that's fine."

"You know, I was glad you didn't stay home that weekend. I looked forward to seeing you, yet by then you knew I was attracted to you. I was even glad you were going alone. At least I got to be with you. I had to keep reminding myself that I had vowed to leave you alone. I didn't keep my resolve completely."

"Well everyone started teasing us and watching us. You were so nice about it, I thought I'd better be a good sport too."

"What else could we do? That bunch got their fun from having someone the brunt of their jokes."

Deb agreed, "Yeah, but they didn't mean harm."

"The trouble was that now you knew I liked you."

"Yes, but you also knew I was married."

"Touche!" He leaned back in his chair. "It didn't stop us from having a good time. I don't remember a lot of the details, but I had a good time, didn't you? I even got to dance with you at the reception."

Deb wasn't sure she should go there now or ever but when one gets older, the risks are easier to take so she said, "Yes...

I remember the first night when we got to the motel in Fargo, do you?"

"Most certainly, but why would you?"

"Why not? Why would I forget?"

"Well, you were married and had a family and a really high-powered life style." Glen reminded her.

"You might think that from your vantage point. But everyone has time to reminisce, dream. I remembered my version the way I wanted to. I'll tell you mine and you can tell me yours. The truth lies somewhere in between." Deb explained.

"That sounds fair." Glen agreed.

"Well, after the drive to Fargo, you in Chris' car and me in Marvin's, we all checked into the motel. As Marvin handed me my luggage from their trunk, you just appeared. My room was upstairs, yours must have been too. You didn't ask, you just said. 'Here, let me take that' and you grabbed it. So I walked beside you upstairs. Do you remember what I asked you as we approached the steps?"

He smiled, "Yes," and they said it together: "How tall are you?" They both laughed.

"Too bad you remember. I wish you didn't. It was a dumb thing for me to say. Guess I was embarrassed about the situation."

"I was flattered that you noticed. I told you how tall I was and then remarked that you were tall for a woman. I found that attractive. Most women came to my waist."

"I offered to tip you for the valet service and you said I could buy you a drink at the bar. Everyone was going there after they took their stuff to their room. Then I got picked on for trying to buy you a drink. It didn't seem to help for me to explain why."

Glen continued, "We all gathered in your room when we left the bar. It seemed natural for the crowd to do that but I wondered if they were babysitting you, sort of protecting you."

"If they were, they wouldn't have all gone off and left you alone with me in my room."

"That was when I should have kept my resolve to distance myself from you. I didn't want to so I just stayed."

"Well, we left the drapes and the door open for all to see. You sat on the chair and I sat on the bed."

"Do you remember what we talked about for hours?"

"No, I don't but I know it was after two before you left."

"Now I'm hurt that you wouldn't remember our intimate conversation." He had to be teasing.

"Sorry, what did we talk about?" She couldn't believe he knew.

He laughed, "no, we talked about growing up on farms and what we experienced as farm kids."

"So that's how you knew I was a farmer's daughter."

"There are stories about farmers' daughters. Some of them not too nice. Are you sure you want to call yourself that?"

"Yes, I'm proud of it, not the stories, but my background."

"It was quite intimate for sure." He teased.

"Well, it might have been. Our farm backgrounds were a common bond."

Dinner courses came and they remarked that the food was delicious. They ordered coffee but no dessert and lingered.

Glen asked Deb, "Do you remember if we ever saw each other again?"

"Yes, I think it was at one of our friend's kid's graduations. I remember seeing you there. Chris and Connie moved away soon after that. Mildred kept me posted on them and added information about you if she knew some. I tried not to seem too interested but I wanted to know about you. She was the one who told me you had moved out east and she told me about you getting married."

"You were interested in me? Why? You were married and had family and a busy life. Surely, my life..."

Deb interrupted him. "I was interested. I thought of you... more than once, more than you think. You were mostly on my thought list, maybe my daydream list once in a while. Why not!" I confessed.

He grinned, a little uneasy. "I thought of you sometimes. I don't know why. There was never any hope of having a relationship with you. You were always married and eventually I was. But I still fantasized about you. Men do that. It's one of our flaws. Guess I can confess that now."

Deb cut in. "Two things you need to know." She held up two fingers. "First, men aren't the only ones who fantasize. Women do it too. Second, you only thought I was happily married. You were dealing with a false assumption."

"I didn't know either one. So women fantasize too, hmm. No, I didn't know that, really. I guess that's the self-centeredness we males have. We think we're the only ones who dream of more than we have, especially when it comes to women." He nodded his head. "I grant you the right to daydream or fantasize." He waved his hand in Deb's direction as if to cast a spell allowing it. "In fact, no, I had better not go that far." He stopped.

"Far, how far? Say it." Deb urged him.

"Mmm, I almost blurted that you could fantasize about me if you wanted to." She started to laugh. "I know" Glen said, "and then I thought that was pretty egotistical of me so I didn't want to finish it. You made me."

"Thank you." Deb laughed. "I will do that, now that I have your permission." Then she asked, "Why are we having this conversation?"

He laughed too. "I have no idea."

⚔ CHAPTER 11 ⚔

THEY'D SAT THERE FOR A COUPLE of hours eating and talking. Glen said "You look tired, Deb or are you relaxed?"

"I am tired and relaxed. Does it show? It has been a long day. I started with my farm chores at 5:30 A.M. remember? They stood up to leave. "The meal was delicious, Mr. Jarvis, thank you."

"The atmosphere was fitting and the company was great."

"Mm huh." Deb agreed. They rode in silence back to her house. It felt comfortable to just be quiet with him. As they pulled up to her house, Deb invited Glen in for a nightcap.

"I'd like that but I don't want to wear out my welcome. Besides, you're tired and you had a long day. There is always tomorrow." Glen reminded her.

"It's only 9:30 P.M. and I won't go to bed yet, anyway." She opened the door of his truck. *I shouldn't have mentioned bed.* She scolded herself. "You don't have to if you'd rather not, you've had a stressful day too." Glen got out following her to the door and held the screen door while she unlocked the inside one. He was so close, she could feel and hear him breathing. Clumsily, she fumbled with the keys.

"May I help?" He offered stepping even closer. The door opened, just then. Deb was relieved, feeling weak. Glen only sat down when Deb motioned him there. He sprawled on one of the love seats while Deb fixed a shot of liquor for them. Handing one to him, she sat down across from him. "Still scared of me?" He teased.

"Could be." She moved over beside Glen.

He grinned. "You know, Deb, I was just thinking, it amazes me that we talk about things like we do. I feel like I dare to say anything to you and it will be ok. And I have!"

"Might be a sign of maturity or just old age." Or maybe time is precious and we can cut the crap, the small talk, and get to the meat of a topic."

"Could be but I'd like to think it's more than that, like we've always been friends in spite of thirty years absence? It's just plain comfortable." He explained.

"It's possible. It's called Filial Love. Deb shared.

"It's what? What is Filial Love?"

"Well, it's brotherly/sisterly love, friendship that you can just take for granted. It's the kind of relationship that takes up where it left off, no matter how long it has been since you were together."

"That's it! How do you know? What is it about?"

"C. S. Lewis wrote many years ago about what he called the four kinds of love. Filial Love is one of them." She explained.

"So what about the others, the rest of them?" He sipped his drink and spread his long legs and arms across the entire sofa, relaxing like he expected to be entertained.

"Sure you want to know all of this? I get going and can't

stop." Deb warned. He smiled and waited. "Well," she began, moving to the edge of the seat and facing him.

First there is Storge Love. It's the love we all have but may not even recognize it as love. Like parents love their children. The child takes it for granted. They both love each other but don't think of it as love. Even when a child screams 'I hate you' at the parent, the child is counting on Storge Love. He knows he really loves his parents and counts on their love. It is a love that doesn't necessarily get loved in return.

It includes things that can't or won't love us back. The touch and smell of a soft, warm puppy, geese flying overhead in the spring and fall, sunrises and sunsets. I love all of them. I love chocolate too but it can't love me back."

"Me too," he added, "chocolate and things I mean."

"You loved your family farm and were reminded of it today. That's Storge Love. Even the memories you cherish are."

He interrupted again. "This is neat."

She continued, "then there is Filial Love. That is where the city of Philadelphia, The City of Brotherly Love gets its name. It includes friendships, gangs, and clubs. Talking over the back fence with good neighbors, coffee friends. We go to church partly to enjoy the community of saints, the gathering together. We don't ask if our friends love us and seldom declare it to them, we just know. We can say anything without fear of being judged or tested. It's comfortable."

"That is what we seem to have. Would you call it chemistry or vibes between two people whether they are of the same or opposite sexes? "

"Yes, I'd say so. There are just some people you are more attracted to and like better than others."

"So tell me about the others since you're an expert." Glen turned toward her.

"I'm no expert, I just remember what I read." She continued. "OK.... The third kind is Eros Love." Glen's eyebrows went up. Deb shook her head and grinned.

"Am I mature enough for this?" He joked.

"Well, I think so. Eros Love is often mistaken for sexual or physical love, sex, even kinky sex. And it can be physical but it is much more. It is the one love we all crave. We think we aren't complete until we experience it. Finding Eros Love is one thing, keeping it is hard work. I always say it is like swimming. You dive into the water but once there you have to change your action. You can't dive again so you must swim or float or tread water so you don't drown. So 'falling' in love is one thing, but once you're in love, you have to change your activity to stay in love. It is frustrating and hard work. Our seminary professor said 'love isn't just blind, it's deaf and dumb too.' He was talking about Eros. This kind of love changes us. We do wonderful things and we are capable of doing horrible or strange things in the name of Eros Love."

"Ah, love."Glen nodded. He was curious. "I need to ask, can one of these loves change or lead to another kind of love? Like could a person have friendship love and then it changes to erotic, romantic love?"

Wondering if he was thinking of us, Deb answered. She felt a flush. "Yes it often does."

Glen leaned forward. "We could stop and go into detail on

this one." he was teasing again, "but you said there were four kinds of love. What other kind?"

"You've heard of it. That's Agape Love." Deb went on.

"Yes, I think it describes God's love for us, right?"

Deb nodded. "Yes, it is God's perfect love, undying, unchanging, always there for us. No matter what we do or how hard we try we can never accomplish loving God or each other that perfectly. We fall short and always let each other down. To love someone so perfectly means we must forgive and forget every time. We often say 'I can forgive and forget but I will always remember.' Our mind won't forget so we can never completely let go and love with Agape Love." Deb quit for a moment, leaning back.

"So you are saying we, any person, I mean, can probably never accomplish this perfect love."

"One can only try. Some relationships come close. A mother's love for her child might. I have seen couples that I thought did, people who," she didn't finish.

"Have you experienced it, this Agape Love? He asked.

Slowly, she answered. "No, not at all. Have you?"

He shook his head and looked thoughtful."No, not that kind of love. I barely. It's hard to explain, isn't it?"

"It's hard to measure love, where one stands in a relationship. It is constantly changing and the individual is only one part of that relationship. When your wife was very ill, you could have come close to Agape Love for her."

"But, I didn't think that." He stopped. "I didn't see it as love but more, probably compassion."

After a few moments, Deb said. "I remember a speaker saying that Agape Love doesn't always feel like love. We don't necessarily decide to love at that level. It's bigger than we are, like she was sick and dying, wracked with pain, not responding, you still loved her enough to stay and see it through. There are people, you know, who abandon the sick person in one way or the other. Myrna, your wife eventually became a person you no longer knew, with her pain and suffering. You stuck it out and cared to the end."

"I would not think of it as love. It becomes duty, devotion, a commitment, the Christian thing to do." Glen was thoughtful about it.

"My dad came close with my mom," Deb shared. "He saw her through all of her illnesses. For forty some years he loved and cared for her and hardly ever got love in return. When she lay dying, her mind was confused and she lashed out at people, especially dad. When she was gone, I thought Dad would be relieved but instead he said 'What at will I do with my evenings now?' For so long, he had cleaned up after work and gone to see her. I wish to think that is Agape Love."

Glen looked compassionately at her. "Yes, I'd say you are right about that."

Deb was near tears from the memory of those days. She had never shared that story with anyone. She cleared her throat. "Have you had enough? Now is where the sermon starts." She joked.

"Preach to me, then!" He folded his hands prayerfully in his lap.

Deb straightened. "I have used the four kinds of love in homilies and speeches a few times.

"Ok, when God created the world, He made it for His enjoyment, just the way He wanted it. God created His humans to have companionship, share love with Him. He gave humans power, dominion, put them in charge of all that He had made. God loved His creation and wanted them to love Him but He gave them free will. God didn't force them to love Him. When they disobeyed God, He still loved them so much that He didn't destroy them and start over, which He could have done. He even went looking for them in the quiet of the evening, like He always did. They were hiding from God, ashamed and aware of their nakedness. He knew where they were and what they had done. God not only still loved them, He gave His most precious gift to them, His Son. He gave His son, Jesus Christ to die for them, for us all, even the ones who refused to love Him. God thought of everything. After Jesus Christ finished being a sacrifice for us, He went home to be with the Father. The Father gave us the Holy Spirit to comfort and keep us until He returns. God's love is so perfect that no matter what we do, He loves us and forgives us. That is Agape Love. End of sermon! Amen."

Glen said "Amen" with her, smiling. "I bet you're good at sermons especially if they aren't any longer than this one."

"Right! Actually, I love writing sermons. To take a text and write about it so that it interests and holds people's attention is really special. I'd rather write sermons than deliver them. I have never fooled myself as to where it all comes from. I am not that cleaver. It is a blessing to be a messenger of the Holy Spirit, to be the go-betweeen."

Glen sat there smiling. "I've never experienced that."

"Yes, you have." Deb argued. "I have seen you set an example for others; praying before eating for instance with disregard that others are there, watching. That is letting the Holy Spirit use you that show you are His. You do it so naturally that you don't think of it as what I call 'Sermons We Give.' It just happens naturally."

Glen was amazed. "You are so insiteful. I would not think of that."

The flush came over her. To cover it up she stood, holding her cup, "More?"

"No, no thank you. You don't take compliments well." He observed. He sat forward and handed her his cup.

Deb felt the flush coming again so she took the cups to the kitchen. That's one of my failings."

"Deb" He stopped until she came back. She sat beside him. "I don't give compliments often. When I do, I mean it. I don't think you realize how special you are. That's appealing in its own way. But a compliment is sort of like a gift. It needs to be acknowledged, at least a 'thank you.' You need to know you are special in so many ways."

"Is this a sermon?" Deb blurted it out. Then she waved her hand "I'm sorry, I didn't mean to make light of it or sound sarcastic. You are right, I don't take compliments well. Thank you for saying nice things to me, about me. I appreciate it."

I didn't mean to scold you, Deb." He put his hand on her arm. "I just want you to know that your knowledge and how you share it so easily is a gift."

"Thank you for that." They both sat looking at each other. *Where do we go from here?* Deb thought.

Glen realized he did care very much. "Deb, I don't want to but I need to go and we both need some rest. This has been incredible." He stood up and took her hand to pull her up. "Really!"

"Will you go back tomorrow?" She asked as she walked him to the door.

"Maybe not. I really don't have to be back until Monday, well, I'll have to leave Sunday. I work Monday."

"Good!." Deb blurted out. *Who said that had anything to do with her?*

"I was thinking today when I was on such a sentimental journey that I haven't been to the International Peace Gardens for at least twenty years, I'd like to drive up there before I leave. I assume it's still there at the border."

"Yes, it surely is."

"Then I could drive by Big Lake and the house we had there where we used to spend summers. You seemed to take all of my time yesterday and today so I didn't have time to go yet."

"Sorry! Then you'd better go tomorrow. I promise I won't stop you." Deb said raising her hands in front of her.

Glen looked pained. "Now that I said that, it's probably a bad time to ask you to go along. No, you wouldn't, I've monopolized enough of your time. You are probably bored with me and the Peace Gardens." He went on with a grin.

"Yeah, right. You just talked me out of it." They both laughed.

"Would you have gone if I hadn't talked you out of it?"

"Yes, but I'd like to be begged now." She teased.

"Ok, I'm begging, will you please go with me? If you won't go, I won't go either. I'll miss it all because of.."

"In that case, I had better go along." She said it in resignation. By now they had walked to his truck. He opened the door and started to get in. Then he turned and in one step had his arms around Deb. She pulled back and kissed him. Then they shared a kiss. He let her go. "Go now." She demanded and pushed him away.

Without protesting he climbed into his truck and pulled the door shut. Then he opened the window. "Good night then!" He seemed startled but started the engine, then asked "what time?"

"Early huh? Come for breakfast. Whenever you get here." She leaned her elbows on the window frame. "I get up early, but how about seven or eight, whenever."

"If it's not too much.." He started to say.

She put her fingers over his mouth. "It's not." She said quietly. He grabbed her hand and held it to his mouth. That feeling deep down inside was back, the weakness. "Go now, I'm tired. I need to go to bed." *I did it again, that bed thing.* She thought as she pulled her hand away and stepped back.

"Deb," he shook his head. Without another word, he drove off.

⚜ CHAPTER 12 ❧

GLEN PULLED INTO A PARKING PLACE at the hotel. He thought about this evening all the way back, not thinking of his driving. This happened earlier when he found himself in Deb's yard. "Get a grip!' he scolded himself. In his room, he undressed and slid under the covers. It was time to rethink this day. He lay there a long time remembering her, her expressions, her touch, the things they had shared in just one day."What is happening here?" He heard himself say out loud. *Don't ask, you know. He felt good but something was confusing about it all. She said we have Filial Love, the friendly kind but I think I'm beyond that. I already dove into the Eros pool. Now I have to start swimming or drown.*

It's like my life just started yesterday. Crazy! He scolded himself. *We're not teenagers so why do I feel like one? I'm sure she feels the same about me, she has to the way she acts. She's the one who kissed me. And then she told me to go as if she were afraid, afraid of me or her. I think of her before I go to bed and as soon as I wake up and dream of her in between. Maybe that's why she tells me to go. She feels it too. She is so totally special. Thank you, God, he prayed.* Finally he slept.

It was a chilly night, the smell of fall was in the air but Deb felt warm walking back to the house. Locking the door, she went straight to her room, dropping her clothes on the floor, she pulled on her nightshirt, and quickly ran her toothbrush over her teeth. She slipped into bed. It seemed cold and dark and big. She grabbed her pillow and hugged it but it didn't hug her back. She still felt the closeness of Glen and the kiss. *I had almost forgotten what it felt like to have a man's arms around me, have him close against me. Sometimes, I ached for that feeling. It had been so long. God, how I wanted to ask him to stay but I was afraid he would.*

It had been a long day, but I still didn't want it to end. I think we did more sharing in one day than I ever did with Dan. "Bonding." We always laughingly labeled it in treatment. What is happening to me?

Lord, I pray, don't let this be just a complication in my life. I don't need that. I haven't had enough of me, for me, just me. I'm not ready. I could feel my sweet, uncomplicated life melting before me. There is nothing missing. I don't need anything else. She argued with herself. *Why can't I just let things happen? Why must I fight it? A few minutes ago, I was basking in the wonderful feeling of having a man care about me and show it. Now, I'm trying to reason myself out of it all.*

Dear Lord, whatever is to be, let Your will be done. Don't let me fool myself into thinking I could love again and then not happen. Whatever happens with Glen, let it be your will. Let it be a blessing to us whether we end up together or not. I am scared, Lord, scared of another relationship, another love. Help me. Amen.

She woke at her usual time feeling anxious so she exercised to loosen up and quickly walked the frontage road trying not to think. The crisp air felt good on her face. She still kept thinking of Glen so she might as well write down her thoughts. She hadn't journaled in several days and a lot had happened. What they say is true that writing bypasses the thinking and reasoning and goes straight to the heart of an issue.

As she wrote, she freely reminded herself of what she 'misses' without a man in her life, her house. The bathrooms are devoid of wet towels, toothpaste in the sink, empty paper rolls, the odor from poor aim around the pot. There are no spots on the mirror or hair clumps in the combs. She doesn't cook unless she wants to and fixes what she likes. When she does, she can fix a lot and eat it all week, which doesn't bore her but probably would someone else. TV doesn't blare with a marathon of sports events that someone may or may not be paying attention to. In fact, silence is a much-appreciated sound a lot of the time. Lights that get turned on get turned off or not by the same person.

She realized how independent and set in her ways she had become in the several years she'd been by herself. *I've always been set in my ways, stubborn. Seldom have I been allowed to have my way while growing up or raising the family. I just did what was required and it left little time for me. I took what I called the "dirty socks on the living room floor" stuff with ease. I cleaned up the messes if I liked and let them lay if not. At the same time I didn't nag about it but might make a remark from time to time that the pile was getting high. Dan would clean them up then.*

At the same time, Dan had to have credit for doing the same. With a houseful of kids and pets he seldom complained. Only once in a while he would suggest they make a path through a room. He hated my piles of "stuff" so he might point at my mess and ask if I could make it into just one pile.

Now, I don't worry about those things. My house isn't always orderly but lived-in. Every pile is mine and I live with it. She wrote for over an hour when it was time to fix breakfast for Glen.

The coffee and sausage were ready and the waffle iron heating when he knocked at the door. Deb started to answer it and the phone rang. She motioned for Glen to come in. "The phone," she said, and waved at him to take a chair at the table. He came in but just stood near her. Pointing to the table did nothing to change that.

"Mom?" Peg asked. "You're finally home!"

"Yes?" Her mother hadn't called her since she had been invited to her house for dinner two days ago.

"Mom, what's going on? What are you doing? I haven't heard from you since Thursday." Deb heard the concern in her voice.

"Well, I've been busy. I had a date."

"For two days! Some date." Peg laughed.

"Well, not the whole time, I've been working too."

"Ok, tell me about your date. Where did you find this guy? You've never seen a guy more than once. This one must be special."

"Well, yes, well, he's a man I knew many years ago," Deb started, looking at Glen. "He came to Grand Island for some business and called me and I went out with him." Glen was smiling, taking in her explanation. He just stood there letting her squirm. She motioned for him to sit. "Pour yourself some coffee," Deb whispered to him with her hand over the receiver.

"Business?" Peg interrupted. "So what kind of business?"

"I really don't know, Peg." She fibbed. "We've had a good time he's been a gentleman," her mother explained.

"So far." Glen whispered and Deb pushed him away.

Peg heard him. "Is he there now at this hour? Mom!"

"Well, yes, we're going to have some breakfast and then drive up to the Peace Gardens. He hasn't been there in a long time."

"Has he been there all night? It's only eight o'clock in the morning!"

"No, of course not, Peg. He just got here."

She interrupted. "Sorry, Mom, it's none of my business. I didn't mean to give you the third degree. You're old enough to do what you want. I'm just concerned. So, where did you say you met this guy?"

"Peg, did I ever tell you about the man who was going to call me for a date many years ago but found out I was married?"

"No! You never did." It sounded like she didn't believe her mother's story and it was going to take awhile to explain.

"Well, he finally got around to calling." Deb started laughing and so did Glen. He had picked up a cup and poured coffee. He enjoyed the attempt she was making to satisfy her daughter. Peg laughed now. "Peg, can we talk about this some other time? The waffle iron is ready and we want to get going."

"Yeah, I want to hear this story, but obviously not now.

Waffles too!" Deb had to stifle a laugh. She put her hand over the receiver and whispered to Glen, "Would you mind meeting them?" He nodded and smiled. Then she said to Peg, "We could stop over when we get back in town?"

"Yes, I'd like that." Peg agreed.

"Ok, it will probably be four or five. I'll take the cell phone and we'll call as we get close to town," planning off the top of her head.

"Ok, Mom, talk to you later. He'd better be nice but at least I can check him out for myself." She sounded satisfied.

"He is, you'll see." They said good-bye and hung up. Deb poured the batter into the waiting iron as Glen looked over her shoulder.

"He is what? What will she see?" Glen asked now sipping his coffee.

"You! What you're like. She worries about me since she lives the closest. She feels responsible. Hope you like waffles. Oh, please sit! You make me nervous."

"Yes, I do; like waffles, I mean." Laughing, he sat finally. "This is delicious, Deb. Mmmm and homemade syrup, huh?" He stopped eating. "It's nice that your daughter cares so much for you. Or don't you like it?"

"It's fine. I appreciate her concern. We laugh about it when either of us gets excessive. Not everyone has a mother in the dating scene. Kind of a reversal of roles but we have a great relationship."

Glen finished one more waffle. Deb cleaned up the kitchen while he filled mugs with coffee for their hour-and-a-half trip. He took the coffee out to his truck. As they settled into the pickup, they agreed the Peace Gardens was a well-kept secret.

❖ CHAPTER 13 ❖

THE INTERNATIONAL PEACE GARDENS IS SPECIAL place of cooperation between the United States and Canada. It is a vast acreage that spans across both borders and both countries support it. It began Deb guessed in the early sixties with a rustic camp for high school kids to come for a week of vocal or instrumental music. Over the years, it grew to a cultural center that allows kids to learn everything that appeals to young, eager talent. Artists, craftsmen, teachers, professors, and conductors join the students to learn more about their interest. All summer, concerts and exhibits go on there. Youth from all over the world come to learn and get to know other students while there. Many come back year after year.

The grounds of the Peace Gardens are truly garden-like. Thousands of flowers and plants adorn the hundreds of acres. Trees, shrubs and orchards are everywhere. Rugged natural woods cover the thousands of acres with hiking trails throughout the grounds. Now, in the fall, most of the leaves have turned or fallen so it looks stark. The evergreens towered above. There are literally herds of deer in the woods. So many deer abound, that several days of hunting are required to limit their numbers so the remaining ones won't starve through the winter.

In a continuing effort to improve the Peace Gardens, organizations join hands across the border to build studios and halls. Large Quonset-type buildings serve as training areas and stages for programs the students perform at the end of their week of study. Summer weekends are a mass of cars, kids and families with suitcases and equipment as kids come for their week and others crowd the grounds and halls for the programs and concerts.

All of it was deserted except for one gift store and snack bar that stays open late into the fall for tourists. The other shops and restaurants were shut down and dorms and practice halls locked up. The interfaith chapel was still open as well as the visitor center. So Glen parked at the top looking out over the gardens that lead to the chapel. They walked down toward the bell tower that looms four or five stories above the chapel. The bell tower stands exactly on the U.S./Canadian border. Glen and Deb took half an hour in the chapel reading the sayings and quotes from people around the world that were etched in stones on the walls. A natural spring usually bubbles up in the center and feeds the fountain when it is on. It creates a soothing effect from its quiet ripple. It was turned off now to preserve it from freezing during the winter months.

Glen paused in front of each carved stone. "Anonymous had to be a wise person, he said. He has quite a few of the quotes here." He looked so serious, it took a moment for Deb to realize he was joking.

"Yes," Deb added. "He had to being quoted so often. Or perhaps it was a she."

The wind was crisp from the north. It stung their faces as they hurried back to the truck. Deb pulled up her hood but Glen only had his bomber jacket so he zipped it tightly and pulled up his collar. The warmth in the truck felt good. Then Glen drove slowly around the grounds. He said he remembered most of the roads were just gravel and there were hardly any parking places. Now most of it was blacktop.

Glen parked the truck near the amphitheater and they walked to a place Deb knew that had been added since the 9/11 Tragedy. Two of the huge beams from the World Trade Towers in New York City had been donated to the Peace Gardens. The twisted shapes and scarred burns were stark reminders of the tragedy. For now, they were just surrounded by posts and ropes. A small sign told what they were. "There are plans to make a fitting spot and memorial with them as a reminder of the lack of peace in our world." Deb told Glen.

Leaving there, they had to stop at Canadian Customs at the border crossing. Glen drove into Dunseith where he stopped at Denby's Café for lunch. It was a mom-and-pop-type place with great burgers and fries and old-fashioned malted milks. There were chunks of ice cream in them. Even though they shared the malt, they were stuffed.

Back in the truck, Glen took a turn off the main highway driving about ten miles toward Big Lake. Deb was just along for the ride so she didn't ask where he was going. He drove past several miles of cottages and homes along the shore slowing finally and pulled into a driveway of a white cottage with green trim. "This was the one that belonged to our family for years."

"Nice," was all Deb said. She wondered if he felt nostalgia about this place too. He didn't say anything for a few minutes but when Deb asked if he wanted to get out, he said, "no. That would be trespassing."

"Don't you want to see the lake? I do."

"Yes, come to think of it, I do. They won't mind if we just walk across the yard, huh?"

"I'm sure not." They walked past the cottage and out toward the lake. The dock was still out so they walked to the end and just stood there taking in the view of the lake. The wind was blowing across the lake enough to cause white caps so they didn't stay long.

"Man, it's cold in this country!" He observed. They hurried to the truck. Glen opened Deb's door, she hopped in and he slammed it. Then ran around to the driver's side and quickly got in. "Cold, wind." He backed out and drove to the highway. He was quiet for a while so Deb just let him be with his thoughts. Then he turned to Deb, "I've been a real case for a shrink with my memory stuff, huh! I thought I might as well do it all while I'm at it. Who knows if I ever get back here again."

"My folks sold the lake cottage after Chris and I were in college. They moved from the farm into Grand Island when Dad retired. I thought they'd enjoy it then but I think it wasn't much fun without kids around. They were happy to live in town and stay there. They spent a couple of months in the south for a few winters but were more content to just stay home."

"I know how they felt. I enjoy traveling and spending time

as a snowbird. I did that a few winters with my sister but I liked being where my stuff was. Home is most comfortable and welcoming for me too".

Our family was like yours. We had a cabin at a lake for about eight years. It was a time when the kids enjoyed boating and fishing and swimming and water skiing. It was a time to get away from being on call. We had a small cabin and a speedboat and pontoon, If Dan couldn't go with us, I'd take the kids. They got up in the morning and put on their swim suits and life-jackets and were safe and happy for the day.

Then the older kids started wanting to do activities that kept them home like getting summer jobs and going to camps. The last summer we had the cabin, we were only up there three weekends. I said it was time to let it go. So we sold it."

Glen shared too."I loved the lake, swimming and boating. We brought friends along and got to know kids around the lake. We went boating and water skiing with them. There were times it was hard to get there because of the farm work during summer. Sometimes, we'd talk Mom into going with us when Dad just couldn't get away. She would but would worry about Dad by himself. She thought she should be there to make meals for him and run errands. When we were older, we could help with the work so Dad could go too. We liked to fish but not unless Dad was along." He looked sideways at her. "Do you like fish?"

"I love to eat it and I hope you do too. I have some to fix for our supper if you do."

"Great! Yeah, I like to fish enough to catch it for eating." He didn't even apologize for making her work to fix a meal.

❊ CHAPTER 14 ❧

CLOSE TO GRAND ISLAND, DEB CALLED Peg. They were home and waiting. Deb assured Glen that he would like her daughter and family.

"Yeah, I heard her give you the third degree about this guy. She'll interrogate me. I'm the man who dominated your time for two or three days and she will want to know all of it. I know."

Laughing at him, Deb said "It won't be that bad."

Peg and Ron's dog, Pica Poo greeted Deb as she came in the door. Once she petted him and spoke to him, he'd be off and leave her alone. This time he had Glen to make a fuss over. Glen let him smell his hand and then scratched his ears making a lifelong friend. Peg and Ron were in the kitchen and after introductions, invited Glen and Deb to sit at the table. Peg offered coffee and set a plate of cookies on the table. Then she sat and got right to the heart of it. "So, you're the guy who has been monopolizing my mother's time." She accused.

"Guilty as charged." He admitted nudging Deb's foot under the table. "I didn't mean to, at least before I called her but we hit it off and one thing led to another. It just happened that way." He left his foot next to Deb's and she liked it.

"That is a pretty vague explanation if you ask me." Peg joked.

"Best I can do without my lawyer present." He shrugged. Everyone laughed.

Then he turned the conversation to Peg. He asked her about her new job. She explained her job as a bank officer. Then she asked Glen about his work. Deb listened too. He told them he was a contracting consultant for a firm that builds factories and office buildings. "No small stuff like houses unless one of us wants the challenge." He finished. Peg was impressed with his carefree attitude and openness. Then he and Ron discovered they had both been in the Air Force, Glen for six years. Ron stayed until retirement two years ago. They swapped service stories and how some things never change in the service.

Deb's granddaughters, Lishal and Susan came in from shopping so Glen launched into a banter with them about school and boyfriends. He teased them until they were laughing. It was easy to see they liked him. He made a hit.

Lishal said. "Grandma, I like this guy, Glen is it? He's neat and has a sense of humor and he's tall too." Turning to Glen, she asked. "How tall are you?" Glen and Deb both laughed and nudged each other's foot under the table. "What?' Lishal asked. "Did I say something funny?"

Glen told her briefly his version of the "how tall are you"story.

When he finished, Deb added, "well, that's his version, anyway." They smiled at each other. Her kids and grand-kids observed closely. Deb wondered if they noticed the sparks between Glen and her. It felt like it was written all over her in everything she said and did. Deb excused herself to the restroom and stood behind Glen's chair when she came back. Glen turned and asked if she was ready to go.

"When you are through charming my grand-daughter." The Grandma joked.

"Are you jealous, Grandma?" Susan teased.

Deb blushed and then tried to get out of it. "No, I'm glad you like each other." But they wouldn't let her get away with it.

Glen got up smiling and searching her face, enjoying the hole she was only digging deeper.

As they walked to the door, Peg asked."Will we see you again, Glen? Soon?"

"I have to go back to the cities tomorrow but sometime." He said looking at Deb for support. She blushed again. Why?

In the truck he asked Deb, "So, what was all that blushing about?"

"I don't know, I just do that sometimes. I hate it when I do."

"I rather enjoyed it. It's sort of refreshing to see someone with modesty these days. I could take that as a compliment." He grinned at her.

"Ok! Enjoy!"Deb made a face at him.

He offered to take her to a movie. "If there is something decent on." Deb handed him the newspaper.

From the kitchen Deb asked. "Is there anything worthwhile?"

"Not really." He recited the list. "Not too appealing, huh?"

"We could rent a movie or you could check my library and see if there is anything you like. I'll cook; you pick out the entertainment, ok?"

"Gotcha!" He replied. Deb showed him where her movies were.

Dinner was parsley potatoes, coleslaw and sliced cucumbers. Glen savored it. "Did you say you caught these fish?" He asked.

"No, a friend who fishes did." *No point in telling him it was about the last package from Dan's supply. If stored in ice, packed in cartons, it keeps for years.*

"Great! Ms. Sullivan, you are an excellent cook!" He complimented her.

"Sometimes, I wonder." She stopped, looking at him. "Thank you, sir."

"Better," he nodded.

"Really, a person gets out of the practice. Besides, I used to cook for a crowd every day. Now I hardly ever cook at all." She offered dessert but Glen refused.

"I will take a rain check later, if I may."

"Sure." Deb got up to clear the table so Glen helped, asking where things went, getting in the way a lot but Deb liked it.

He had picked out an old movie from the fifties, *The Greatest Show on Earth.* "I know I've seen it but can't remember. Charleton Heston, right!"

Deb tried to remember. "Hmm and Betty Grable and Jimmy Stewart. I can't remember the others. Ah, Louis Jordan, no someone else like him. I haven't seen it in a long time. But I like the story." She plopped into her recliner and raised the footrest.

"I'd make room for you here." Glen noticed as he moved to the end of the sectional.

"I need to put my feet up, they're tired, from all that cooking." She said turning on the TV and starting the tape.

"If you sit here, you can put your feet up here." Glen offered, patting the spot next to him. So she moved over next to him being aware of that feeling inside when she was close to him. He reached for her feet, took her shoes off. "Oofda!" He made a face.

"Ok." She started to pull away.

"No." He laughed, pulling her feet back. The movie was starting so they settled back. He rubbed and massaged her feet. It was wonderful, to the point of distraction.

"Umm." Deb groaned.

"Hurt? Am I hurting you?" He asked.

"No, not at all." She admitted. "It's just wonderful, that's all."

"Good." He rubbed for a minute more and the movie distracted him. She reached for the throw beside her to cover her feet.

"If you feel chilly, there's a throw behind you." She leaned toward him to reach it. He got it and began to spread them both out. "I'll get another one." Deb turned for that one.

"We can share." He said as he pulled her closer beside him and smoothed the covers over them both.

"There is another one." Deb gestured and laughed. He ignored her, intent on tucking them in, pulling her even closer. It wasn't easy stretching them that far if you considered how long they both were. He reached around in front to get the other one. Deb held her breath as his face came so close. That feeling was there again.

I'm not sixteen. She silently scolded herself. He pulled the third afghan around their shoulders. He found her hand under the cover and tucked it closer and held it. With feet on the coffee table and slouched down it was cozy enough to concentrate on the movie. He caught her dozing toward the end. When she opened her eyes, he smiled and squeezed her hand. He was so comfortable to be with.

The movie ended and they tried to remember the actors so they waited for the credits at the end. The movie was made in1951. "I was in the seventh grade, then." Glen said.

"You're younger than I. I was in the ninth grade."

Glen sat up straight, acting as if he were shocked. "You mean you're older than I am? I don't know if I can handle this!" He teased.

"Well! I could just be the older woman in your life." Deb started to get up.

He grabbed her arm and pulled her back. "No, I like older women. They have more experience, life experience that is." He grinned. "Now you offered me some dessert. Are you up to getting it ready for me?"

"Probably not! I'm too old to handle it this late at night."

"Don't do it if you have to leave to do it. Here, I'll help." He got up and followed her.

Deb laughed as she pulled away and headed to the kitchen. "Would you like coffee with it?

"No thank you. Pie is enough."

She handed him his pie and sat beside him. "This is very good. "He said.

"Its key lime pie, goes well with fish."

"Not just the pie, all of this is very good." Glen declared.

"Yes." She agreed. "It has been quite a last few days. I have enjoyed it."

"Yes." He leaned back. "yes, me too. We do have some issues though like you being an older woman, and being loose enough to meet with a married man. That and a more serious situation. We live so far apart."

Deb took his plate. "It's more serious than that. I waited thirty years for you to call me for a date. I don't think I can wait another thirty for you to call again. I probably won't be dating at the nursing home." She got up to take their plates to the kitchen.

"Hey! That's not fair! You were married the last time I wanted to call you. You come back here!" He was nearly shouting. He started laughing.

Deb came back and plopped down beside him, laughing with him. He put his arm around her and she leaned her head on his shoulder. They were still for a moment. She spoke. "You will leave tomorrow for sure, huh?"

"But," his breath close to her hair. "I could still see you in the morning, that is if you're not sick of me. I could go to church with you. Do you go early?"

Deb sat up beside him. "Yes, I go at eight o'clock. I would like to have you go with me."

"Would it cause you any embarrassment?" He asked seriously.

"Absolutely!" Deb joked. "Depends on what you wear, how you behave, etc. What do you have in mind?" He grinned and shook his head. "Seriously, yes, it will cause a stir. I belong to these people. They are my family. But I really don't mind." She peered at him. "It might be interesting."

"Yeah, I forgot. You're The Church Lady there. Oh, me." He shook his head.

"It's OK, Glen, really." Deb assured him. "I could come and get you."

"Good." Glen stood up. "I don't want to but I should go now. Seems like I've said that before." Deb walked him to the door and they stopped. "Deb, thank you for the meal, meals and your family and you. I, ah..." He said under his breath as if talking to himself. "I want to say.." He stopped. "That was dumb." He stepped close and touched Deb's cheek. She felt weak. "You bother me!" He tried to explain."I get all tongue-tied and don't say what I want to when I am close to you. Then I think of it when I get back to the hotel." Glen looked confused.

"So give me a call." Deb wanted so badly to laugh but she didn't dare. She couldn't help smiling. She felt the same.

"You're laughing, aren't you?" He accused her. "You are! You're enjoying this!"

Deb laid her hand on his arm. "I'm not laughing at you, honestly. I'm laughing at both of us." She couldn't hold back any longer. "Glen, I know it's hard to explain." Deb tried to stifle her laugh."We are pathetic"

He grabbed her arms, turned her to face him. Now he was chuckling. He leaned against the door, pulling her with him. "Thank you, Deb for this and the whole weekend. This has been unforgettable."

Deb wished she dared tell Glen. She didn't want it to end but was afraid she'd tell him to stay and not be able to handle it. He put his arms around her and they kissed several times. Deb pulled away from him. "You have to go! Go, or I won't let you, please." Glen looked shocked. "I'll pick you up by around seven thirty in the morning." Deb said.

He opened the door, turned back and kissed her again. "Ok, good night."

Deb shut the door, shaken, aching to call him back, then she heard his truck roar up the driveway.

❧ CHAPTER 15 ❧

GLEN WOKE SUNDAY MORNING REMINDED THAT he had gone to sleep wishing he had Deb in his bed. *Why is it that men always think in terms of physical attraction? I even dreamed she was here beside me in bed. It wasn't even a sexual dream, just sensuous. I don't ever remember having such a dream.* He just lay there shaken not wanting to break the spell.

Since I'd been alone, I had more than a few offers to go to bed with a woman, single or not. But I seldom felt even tempted. I had urges I wanted to satisfy but I was sure it wouldn't help if I had no real feelings for any of them so I passed them up. Cowardice had a lot to do with it, I think. But none in eight years ever appealed to me. I certainly never dreamed of them.

She's different from Myrna or any other women I know. He thought as he lay there. *Married to Myrna was pleasant enough. We were compatible and agreeable most of the time but there was something missing. There were times when I wanted more passion, more depth, whatever one would call it. Myrna was a kind, pleasant, loving person to me and the kids. She gave it as much as I expect and I loved her in many ways, there was just something missing. I often blamed it on being a ready-made family and older when we married.*

It's not that I regretted marrying her. But my daydreams did. I knew couples who had more "spark" even after many years of marriage.

After Myrna's illness and death, I swore I would never marry again. I plan never to go through that again. I was there through her suffering. Cancer was a wicked trick of nature that turned a beautiful person into a tortured, degraded skeleton. At the end everyone was relieved. I reasoned, I would never marry again. So I'd be free from what I went through with Myrna.

He rolled over, looked at the clock. It was six thirty.

Deb, so what about Deb? Explain that. Thoughts of her overshadow my resolve. Do I just go to bed with her, satisfy my urges? I finally found a woman who turns me on enough to even think about it. Is it wrong to love and be loved and express it at our age? Maybe it would eventually lead to marriage. It does in books and movies and tv. A lot of people do it and think it's ok.

Am I kidding? I couldn't do that with any woman I care about. If I loved her that much, I would love her enough to marry her. Guess I'm just old -fashioned. So do I resign myself to never loving again?

"Ooff!" He exclaimed out loud. He got up, showered, shaved and dressed. *I'm glad I brought a suit.*

His mind just wouldn't let his argument go. In the shower, he thought, *so would I change my mind for the right person? Would I really marry again and risk watching her suffer and die?*

Then again, I'm only in my sixties. I could have twenty or more years to be alone or with someone. It would have to be the right person. Would they be quality years facing old age with body parts wearing out with aches and pains? I've already started that. Would it be easier, more comforting with someone or alone?

After all of these years I thought I was used to being alone. I admit I still miss someone to sit across the table from at mealtime and someone to say "good morning" or "good evening" to. The only time I miss a mate is going places especially on trips with my friends. They make me feel welcome all day but they have someone to go home with or to their room with. I go alone.

Glen stepped out of the shower, wrapped the towel around his waist and shaved. Peering into the mirror, he took stock of the thinning hair and lines that were growing around his mouth and eyes. New lines were appearing on his forehead, worry lines. *That's what they call them.* He thought. *They are a result of Deb. She disturbs me. Imagine having her around all day.* He chuckled. Time to get dressed.

❧ CHAPTER 16 ❧

DEB WOKE AND STRETCHED INTO THE corners of the bed remembering the feeling of Glen close to her, his embrace, his kiss. *I wish he were here now doing it again. In this bed? Mmm, don't go there. Only one person has ever slept in this bed and that is I. I call it my "virgin bed" because noone but me has slept in it since the day I bought it. It still is. I even joke that after ten years of no sex, a person must be a virgin again. I hug my pillow but it doesn't hug me back.*

The clock was at five thirty, *two hours until I have to leave. Wonder what kind of stir it will cause when I arrive with a man no one knows.* She slipped on her robe and went to the mailbox for the newspaper. Out here in the country, a person could go out in nothing and no one would know or care. It was dark and chilly this morning.

She rushed inside anticipating the warmth, poured juice, warmed a muffin, and sat at the table with the paper. Suddenly, it was time to get ready. She found herself dressing for Glen, hoping he'd like her royal blue dress and velvet jacket. It had been a long time since she dressed with a man's approval in mind.

As she pulled up under the portico of the hotel, Glen came out of the door. He looked good in a navy suit and red tie. *I'd be proud to go to church with him.* She thought as he reached the car in several steps, opened the door and arranged his long legs in her van.

He turned to Deb."Hi."

"Good morning! You look neat in your navy, very nice." Deb noticed.

"Morning! Thanks, you look very nice too. What a couple, huh?" He blurted and stopped.

As Deb parked by the church, Glen touched her arm. "Deb, I need to talk to you after church, before I leave, ok?"

"Sure, ok." She answered. They went into the church and sat before a lot of people came. Deb preferred the front where it was easy to leave by the side door. But that meant they'd be in full view of most of the congregation. Peg, Ron and the girls joined them in the pew. They leaned forward to say good morning and smiled knowingly.

Sharing a hymnal, Glen and Deb's fingers touched now and then. Deb remembered a time so very many years ago when she did the same thing with another man she loved. It was hard to concentrate. Glen had a deep pleasant voice and sang well. She wondered if he sang in the choir, a requirement on her imaginary list of qualifications for a husband.

Her hypothetical list, was a family joke. Deb's next husband had to be a dancer, singer, have a sense of humor, be a conversationalist, a conservative and Christian and leave the curtains open to let the sun and outdoors in. Her daughters had added a few more items. He had to like hockey and have never been convicted of a felony. The check list was brought up if she saw a man more than once.

Reaching past Glen, she took a communion card from the back of the pew. He noticed and smiled. She showed it to him and whispered. Do you want to commune?" He nodded so she handed him one and whispered again, "Hand it to the usher when we go up." He shoved it in his shirt pocket and grinned. "No!" She whispered, nudging him. "Fill it in for the record."

He pointed up. She knew what he meant and poked him again shaking her head and stifling a laugh. Finally, he wrote something on the card. Then offered to show it to her. She squeezed his hand and tried to give him the look she gave her kids when they misbehaved in church. He returned a look that she would often get from a kid. Lisal was sitting next to her Grandma. She leaned forward and whispered, "do we have to separate you two or can you behave?"

Members smiled and greeted them on the way out of church. Deb introduced Glen to some of them and just said good morning to others. Of course the pastor at the door wanted to know his name and where he was from, etc. Outside at last, Pegs kids invited them to breakfast with their family. But Deb said Glen had to get going. She was accused of monopolizing Glen.

On the way back to the hotel, Deb asked Glen if he had time to eat. "Yeah, how about at the hotel? They have a buffet that wouldn't take time. "He said "Let me put my bags in my truck and check out. Come with me. I need to talk to you."

"Me, in a man's hotel room? On Sunday? What will my church people say? You already think I am slut, an old slut." They laughed. She went along. They stood there waiting for the elevator and she felt conspicuous enough.

Glen whispered from behind Deb "Everyone is looking at you, the Church Lady, Sinful!" And then he laughed.

Deb was relieved when the door shut behind them. Glen went into the bathroom to change. He came out, he packed his suit in his bag and put on his leather bomber jacket. He looked good in it. Deb didn't tell him. She sat on a chair and watched. He sat on the bed across from her, knees nearly touching.

"Deb, I want to ask you a question. Would you come to the cities to visit me?"

All through church Deb wondered what he wanted to say and was relieved yet a bit disappointed. Her romantic side had something else in mind. "Yes, Glen. I'd like that."

"Good!" He looked relieved. "We could go to a game, a show, whatever you'd like to do. I'll send you a plane ticket. I don't want you to drive that far alone."

"Glen, you don't have to do that. I can.."

He interrupted. "Deb, I want to if you'll let me. I'll make your plane reservations and a motel one too. I want you to come and visit and just be with me." He hesitated and stammered. "I don't want you to get the wrong idea. Just come for fun."

She said "Ok."

"Well, I want to be with you, friends, whatever." He talked as if to convince her and Deb had already said "yes". He went on, "I know, I want to see you again. I suppose we need to be cautious but I want to see you, be with you. If I'm rushing you, well, I don't want to waste time either. Does that make sense?" He stopped and sighed. "Am I going on and on with my sales pitch?"

Deb couldn't help but laugh. "I said 'yes' so you don't have to. But here we are over the hill and we worry about being cautious and taking time. It is the one thing we don't have a lot of."

"Just being with you is, having you here with me in this room, it gives me ideas that, well you will need to stay somewhere else."

"Ok, I understand." Deb agreed.

"Well, when could you come?"

"Soon." Deb moved to sit by him on the bed and took out her calendar. Comparing schedules, they decided on the third weekend in October.

"It seems far away." Glen sounded disappointed.

"It's only three weeks." Deb assured him.

"Can you come on a Friday morning and go back on a late Sunday flight? It would be almost three days. I know you work."

"My job is really flexible. As long as I see my people regularly and the pastors can cover the hospitals, I am free to go when I like. My job is not a problem." Deb stopped and stared at Glen. "You, Mr. Jarvis, are complicating my life."

"Deb, I don't want to interfere with your time you need. We could just be friends and be together. Have someone to go places with instead of being alone. It could be whatever we make it."

She shook her head. "That wouldn't work for me." He

looked stunned. "I tried that once Glen, having a friendship with a man. It was the hardest work I ever did to be 'just a friend.' At the time, we were both married and anything but a friendship was impossible. It got more difficult I was single."

"Well, we're both single." He said. "We are free to do what we want with our relationship. We seem to just click. I think it would be fun and interesting to continue."

"Scares the daylight out of me!" Deb declared. "Yet, what do we have to lose? For now, I can hardly wait to come to the city to be with you." Deb stood up. So did he. She looked him in the face. "This looks like a lot more work!" He folded her in an embrace that made a sob escape and he stepped back to look at her face.

"Deb?"

Being sensible, Deb said. "We need to eat and get you on the road." She started for the door. That strange feeling, she had to get out of this room but could hardly walk straight.

Glen noticed. "Are you ok?" He turned and grabbed his bag off the bed. "Deb?" She steadied herself with the door handle, then opened the door and stepped into the hallway. Inside the elevator, she took some deep breaths. Glen kept watching her, looking confused. "Are you all right?" He asked as they stepped out.

"I'm fine." Was all she could say. Glen stopped at registration, ran his bag out to his truck while Deb waited and they went to the buffet in the restaurant. They didn't talk much. Deb wasn't hungry.

Glen walked her to her car. He opened the door and kissed

her good-bye before she got in. "I'm glad I called you, Deb. I can't remember having such a wonderful time."

"Me too. I never expected to see you again after so many years." She kissed him again and got into her car. "Now go, good-bye."

"I'll call you." Glen promised as he shut the door.

Deb rolled down the window. "They all say that!"

He smiled, waved and turned to his truck. Deb started to back out and he disappeared in opposite direction.

⚜ CHAPTER 17 ⚜

DEB WAS GLAD IT WAS A warm day. She spent it doing yard work. The sun soothed her skin. She was *reminded of Glen, his warmth.* She got her flowerbeds ready for winter but couldn't bring herself to tear out flowers that were still blooming. She enjoyed digging in the dirt and pruning the plants. *I was happy with my life alone. I convinced myself that life was complete. Since Dan died. I've had my work, my friends, my family. I had peace that I hadn't known for many years. That was all I needed or could ask of life.*

Now this man comes into my life and makes me think differently. Where, how will he fit in? We have no pretenses. We willingly risk showing our feelings and emotions. I don't know him that well. But, I don't think I can be "just a friend" to Glen. It didn't work with Fred Anderson. Maybe it did and we didn't admit it. Friendship was all we could ever have. We are still friends. I don't hear from him for months and then he calls or writes.

We never did go further than a hug. I kissed him on the cheek one time as a 'thank you' gesture but that was all. It was agonizing to be on guard to be just friends.

With Glen I'm comfortable not worrying about that. We're both unattached, available so we have the freedom to be whatever we are to each other. It's only been ,well almost two years for me, maybe I'm not ready. But Glen has been alone for eight years. He might be set in his ways by now.

I really don't need another friend. So what do I need? I crave passion, romance, sex, physical and emotional, real, meaningful love. I need a "good romp in the hay." What else? I want companionship, compassion, a male best friend who wants to be with me. A man whom I would watch football with and he would go to a musical with me just because we loved each other enough to please each other. Either that, or I'll just stay the way I am. Perhaps, I am asking for too much. It may be impossible.

Though, I'll never settle for less. I settled for less with Dan, never again. I reached the point with Dan where I chose not to show physical or any other affection for him. If I couldn't have all of a marriage, I chose to have none. Our marriage ended long before he died.

Glen said he will settle for friendship. We could settle for an affair. Would it be enough or would it spoil everything between us? From experience, Fred and I never went there, we agreed it was wrong and would cost us a lot family-wise. But he was afraid it would be over for us if we just once gave in. He said he would never be able to face me again. I argued once wouldn't be enough and our double life would eventually destroy what we had. We never found out. .

How about sex? I know a lot of people who never worry about making their relationship permanent or legal. They just do as they want or need to. Could we do that? What might Glen expect? I don't know what he wants from me, for us.

Can I give up my privacy, my independence? Is any man worth that/

Peg stopped over so Deb took an iced tea break from her thoughtful argument and gardening. "Mom, do you want to tell me some more about this guy, Glen? You seem very compatible. Actually, the word is more like smitten, like, in love maybe?"

"Peg, we really do like each other. I know at my age this is crazy, but I, I think I'm in love." It scared her to say it out loud. She looked at Peg for her reaction. She surprised her mom and only smiled. "Doesn't it shock you or surprise you? Say something." Deb started to laugh.

Peg reached over and hugged her mother. "Mom, if Glen is as nice as he seems and you can be as happy with him as you seem, I think it's wonderful. You've got twenty or thirty years to have each other. So what will you do with that time? Where do you go from here?"

"I just don't know. We are both in shock. We're too old for this."

"Mom, you've been love-starved for too many years. Go for it."

"Well, I'm going to spend a weekend there next month." Peg raised her eyebrow. "I'll stay at a motel. We'll just play together during the day, ok?"

"It's okay with me, Mom. You're old enough to take care of yourself, I hope."

⚔ CHAPTER 18 ⚔

EVERY MILE BACK HOME GLEN THOUGHT of Deb and this weekend. *I feel overwhelmed by my feelings for Deb and what I planned to do about them. I argue with myself trying to sort it out. Even though I'm confused, I feel good.* He even found himself praying that the Lord's hand was in this turn in his life. He felt less a struggle after he prayed yet no clear answers came.

It is a special love, like I've never known, not even with Myrna.

"What am I doing? I'm not a teenager but that's how I feel. At my age, I shouldn't be thinking this way or feeling like this." He thought out loud. *What will I do with this new love? The real question is what Deb will do about it. He was sure she had feelings for him, but he also knew she loved her privacy and freedom. Would she love him enough to give that up for a life of companionship and sharing?*

I'll take her on any terms she is comfortable. Only three weeks and we will continue this, whatever it is.

Glen called Deb as soon as he got home. He felt good when he heard her "Hello."

He was tired from the trip but felt a surge of energy

knowing she was there for him. "Hello, did you know it was I this time?"

"Yes! Not exactly, but I thought you might be home by now and I wished I had asked you to call me when you arrived safely."

"I thought you'd think I was being a pest or I might have called you on my cell phone while I was traveling. I had this feeling of being pulled farther away like a rubber band that can only stretch so far and it will spring back or break. But it didn't, and now I'm here and you are there."

"Mmmm, I like that."

"I don't."

"I don't mean that you're there and I'm here but just the picturesque way you put it. In three weeks, your rubber band can relax."

"I thought a lot about you, us while I drove all day. Like, what I am going to do about you?" He stopped. "What did you do without me to monopolize your time?"

"I worked outside. I was grateful for the warmth of the sun. It reminded me of how you warmed the last few days for me."

"I like that, thank you." It was easier to say these things over the phone. "Well, I need to bring my stuff in and then go to bed. I have to work tomorrow. I'll call you after I talk to the travel agent, ok?"

Deb felt a twinge hearing the fatigue in his voice. "Yes, call in the evening or use my cell number. I'm up late but I don't mind if you wake me."

He didn't share his thoughts. "I'll let you go now."

"Glen, I'm glad you called me." They said "goodbye" and hung up.

Monday Deb usually didn't go in the church. That was her morning to make phone calls, set up visit times and make rounds at the nursing homes in the afternoon. She decided she'd better go to coffee time today just to get it over with. Sure enough! "Who was the fellow with you? He's tall, a lot taller than you are even. How tall is he? So is this your new boy-friend? Looked serious! What's his name? Where is he from? Where did you meet him?" They all blurted out over each other.

Deb held up her hand to stop them. "One at a time." She declared. "That's why I came today, I knew I'd have to defend myself eventually. He's a guy I knew some thirty years ago. He came to town on business and called me. That's all."

"Is it serious? Is this THE guy? What business did he have, monkey business? How serious is it?"

"I'll let you know, you'll be the first," She lied and they knew it.

"But," the pastor said in his slow authoritative manner. "It must be serious if you bring him to church with you."

"I thought that was in the olden days." Deb tried to protest.

"Oh, goodness no," he went on. "Now-a-days when you bring a member of the opposite sex to church, it is serious. Why it is the first step before coming for marriage counseling."

"I don't think so." She said unbelieving. Everyone in the coffee room laughed. He was just teasing her wasn't he?

"Yes, this is a serious sign." Everyone agreed with him.

"Well, don't count your marriages before they hatch." Deb

paraphrased. They all laughed. "Think of how many 'never-agains' I'd have to eat if I decided to marry again."

"A lot if I recall." The janitor reminded her.

"Where is he from and where did you find him?" Bev, the secretary wanted to know.

"He's from the Twin City Area and I met him over thirty years ago. He came to Grand Island for business and decided to call me so we went out. He's just a friend." Deb explained.

"Friend, yeah," they all agreed but she didn't think they were convinced.

She found herself telling the story of their first encounter again. The church staff was so thrilled, you'd think it happened to each of them.

Glen woke early with Deb on his mind. This was getting to be a habit. He might as well go to his office early. Traffic was lighter then and he had several days of mail to read. He was about finished when Barb, his secretary opened the door. "Hi, boss." She popped her head. "Why so early today?"

"I just thought I'd get started on the mail." He explained.

"How was your weekend in North Dakota? Did you call that woman you told me about?" Barb was standing by the door. She looked closer."Is there something different about you? You look brighter, rested, something, younger. I don't know what it is." She shut the office door behind her and made a beeline for the chair near his desk as if to get an exclusive. "Tell me now. What happened to you?" She leaned forward.

"None of your business, what happened."

Not giving up she pressed on, "The fresh air, no, something

happened, I can tell." She tilted her head, looking quizzically at him.

He grinned. "It was wonderful weather, quiet, no crowds, away from work and traffic. So I got rested up."

"No, that's not all. There's something more. I have a right to know. After all, I am your private secretary." She begged.

"Not that private." He laughed. "Ok, I got a new hairdo, now you know. I just can't keep secrets from you."

"You did call her." She wouldn't give up.

"Yes, I did call her." He felt himself flush.

"Boss," she teased pointing her finger at him. " You met up with that woman. I can see it in your face. What..." she started. "No, it's none of my business. You're right! I won't ask you but I know it worked out. Something happened, I can tell. You look great. I'm so happy for you." She ran on.

"Calm down, Barb. I did see her and we spent some time together, yes. That's all." He could still feel the flush.

Barb stood and became serious. "Well, I hope it works out for you, boss. You deserve a good relationship."

"Thanks, Barb." That was all he planned to say for now. If he was that transparent, how would he get through coffee break with his partners? He dreaded it but knew he had to show up or it would be worse.

Everyone in the coffee room started in on Glen. "Hmm, could he have gotten a tan up north this weekend or is he blushing? He looks different, younger, his eyes are shining. Maybe he won the lottery. Don't have one in that state." They went on and on like he wasn't there. Finally, they stopped and started laughing.

"Barb, did you..." he started.

"No, boss, honestly, I never... I just told them what you told me that you got a new hairdo." Everyone roared.

"Are you done now?" Glen asked smiling.

"Did you fall in love or what?" Jim Kress, his partner and best friend asked.

"Or what!" Glen answered. "Is there no privacy in this world?"

"Well, we should be the first to know." His other partner, Greg Masterson chimed in.

"Oh, you will be. He lied thinking of his plans for the next three weeks. He'd already called his travel agent and wanted to go home so he could call Deb about it tonight. The office staff continued harassing him all day.

He called Deb as soon as he got home. She was fixing herself something for supper. He hadn't even thought of food yet and he told her so.

Deb felt a twinge of sadness that he was home alone and had to fix his own supper, the care giver in her. She approved his travel plan. He said the tickets would be electronic so she just had to get them at check-in at the airport at 5 A m on the twenty-third. He'd also made reservations for her at a nearby motel. The other reservations he said were a surprise. He'd asked what she enjoyed doing but she had left it up to him. Deb said it wasn't necessary to schedule all of the time. It would be nice to just be together. He told her they'd have time for that too.

They called each other every few days to share news. It

seemed like they could say how they felt more easily on the phone and never ran out of things to say.

Deb thought she'd better call her daughter Carol in Nebraska and confess her latest activity. Though Carol lived the farthest away from her, Deb was close to her. Deb told her about her weekend and how she had known Glen before. Carol was happy to hear that her mother had a date, and teased her about going to see him for an entire weekend. Deb assured her it would be respectable, though she wasn't convinced herself.

"I'm not worried Mom. You're a big girl now. I just don't want you to get hurt. Mom. I love you and want you to be happy."

"I'll keep that in mind." She admitted it was scary. Carol warned her though, "if you continue this relationship, Mom, you have to give me a chance to meet him too. I have a right to make a first hand judgement."

Peg came over Thursday night before Deb was to leave for the cities. She sat on the bed and watched as her mom packed and unpacked. She wanted to take as little as possible so she could just carry everything on the plane. "Mom, you have a special glow, a look that I've never seen on you. Are you in love with this guy?"

Sitting on the bed beside her, Deb confessed, "Peg, I have strong feelings for him. I really think I could get serious about him. I didn't want to at first, but the longer I know him… the more we are apart… I can hardly wait to hear his voice on the phone. And we never seem to have enough time to say it all. We are so compatible. I am really looking forward to this weekend."

"I like him, Mom and I could see how you treated each other, that you have something special. Be careful, Mom, but be happy too. You deserve it." Reaffirming that Ron would drop her off at the airport on his way to work in the morning. They hugged each other good bye. "I love you, Mom" she called as she got into her car.

⊰ CHAPTER 19 ⊱

EVERYONE IN GLEN'S OFFICE FOUND OUT he was having "that woman" come for the weekend. They spent another day teasing him. He told his partners, Jim and Greg and his secretary, Barb about Deb.

He left work early Thursday afternoon to get ready for his guest. He made sure his housekeeper, Mary knew he had company coming. She excitedly cleaned extra well. She baked cookies and muffins for him. She usually grocery shopped for him but Glen wanted to do it. He bought fruit, snacks and cappuccino mix and a liquor for a chilly evening. At the checkout he bought flowers in packages to give his place a fresh look. He didn't tell Mary it was a female visitor but she had worked for him since he moved to his townhouse. She could read him easily by now.

It only took an hour to fly from Grand Island to the Twin Cities. The plane landed and Deb grabbed her suitcase from the bin above her and adjusted her travel bag over her shoulder. She saw Glen as she approached the escalator. He was leaning against the wall.

Deb felt giddy as she made her way to him. He stayed there until she came through the crowd and suddenly he was in front of her. He swept her into his arms, bag, suitcase and all. Deb hugged him back. "What's this?" He asked noticing her bags.

"I didn't want to have to go to baggage claim so I carried everything on."

"My kind of traveler!" He said as he grabbed her suitcase and her hand. They began the long walk to parking. "Seems I've done this before" he smiled at her, "carried your luggage."

"Yes, I believe so." Looking up at him, she asked. "How tall are you?" He squeezed her hand.

He walked her to a gray Buick sedan. "The truck, where is it?" She asked.

"Oh, this is my car to pick up lovely ladies at the airport in." He teased. He put the suitcase in the trunk and gently took her shoulder bag and gestured to put it there too.

"Sure." Deb agreed. Then he reached for the door on the passenger side of the car. They were in each other's arms. She staggered back against the car with him falling against her. "Glen" she whispered losing her breath.

He stepped back. "Sorry, did I hurt you?" Pulling her away from the car, he opened the door and Deb gratefully fell in. In the driver's seat, Glen leaned over and kissed her, then took her hand, smiling. "I've missed you. It seemed like more than three weeks."

Deb leaned back on the seat, relaxed now. "I missed you too." She slid her hand under his. Neither of them spoke again until he turned into a housing area with large trees at the entrance and a sign that read "Evergreen Estates." Then she sat up and looked. "Beautiful!" The road ran between a beach area next to a small lake and town-houses for about half a mile.

Glen turned into a driveway. "Here we are," he announced as he stopped in the driveway. She was shocked but tried to conceal it. This was the house, the one she always wanted to have. She had the plans for it still even after giving up years ago of having one. It was incredible!

They got out and went onto a deck that spread on two sides of a brown A frame town-house with glass going all the way into the peak. They entered through large sliding glass doors into a huge room. The east wall of the house had a stone fireplace. It dominated the whole two stories of the room. In front of the fireplace sat a large plush sectional and a glass-topped coffee table about six feet long. A giant recliner that surely must fit Glen sat at one end. It was surrounded by a lamp and table with stacks of reading material around it. It looked comfortable and lived-in. Across the room on the west, was the dining area in front of the wall of glass. Deb noticed the drapes were open toward the lake as they should be. The kitchen was in the wall on the north end and beside that was an open stairway with an oak railing that curved to the top. She stood there looking and made a complete circle before she noticed Glen watching her. He smiled at her reaction. He knew she approved.

"Glen, it's wonderful! It's, I'll tell you later. It's great!"

"Come on, I'll show you the rest." He took her hand and led the way to the hall between the kitchen and stairway. There was a utility room with a door into the garage. He opened it and his truck was there. Another small room was across from it. "This was supposed to be my office at home but I never got past bookshelves with boxes on them. Someday."

"Uh huh!" Deb smiled up at him. Clearing his throat, he took her arm and led her down the hallway.

"This is my room!" He announced. "His room" was a large master bedroom done in blues and greens. The king-sized bed dominated it. A door led to a dressing room with built-in drawers and shelves. Past that was the bathroom with a hot tub. A glassed-in shower stall was in the corner and one wall was a solid mirror. Two sinks with a long counter were separated from the toilet by a wall.

"Very nice. Did you design this yourself?" She asked.

"Yes, this part of the house wasn't finished when I found it so I got to design it myself. That is why my office is small. It got crowded out by my large bathroom but I like it this way."

"Me too. You did a great job designing and decorating. I am impressed."

"I wondered if you'd like my place." He took her by the elbow. "Come on, I'll show you upstairs and then we'll have something to eat. I'll take you to your motel afterward. We have a full day."

They climbed the stairs. Each step was covered separately in a plush cream carpet. There was an open balcony with an oak railing overlooking the living area below. A room with a bath was the first one at the top of the stairs. There was little furniture, not even a bed. "I meant for this to be a guest room but I hardly ever have company so wasn't in a hurry."

"Right." Deb agreed.

The room at the end of the hallway did it for Deb. She was

in love with Glen's house. There was glass up into the peak of the roof. French doors led to a balcony with a view of trees and a large building in the complex area. He had a desk and rocking chair in it but that was all.

"What a marvelous room and you don't use it?" She asked, disbelieving.

"I have enough space downstairs for me, for one person. But yes, it is a neat room, a lot of potential. You can have it." He waved his hand as if to make it so.

"Thanks!" Deb wondered if he meant it.

They went back downstairs. Glen seated Deb at the table where she could look out at the trees that were just turning colors here. The lake was still and dark blue in the background. He turned on the coffee and brought fruit, muffins and juice to the table. After a prayer, they ate and talked .

"Glen, this is so beautiful, the house, the trees and lake. It's great!"

"I like it too." He looked at the clock. "We have to go. Stay dressed as you are. It'll fit our fun for today." Grabbing the food and dishes from the table, they quickly put them away, bumping into each other in the kitchen as usual. It was fun.

They hopped in the car, stopping first at the motel "We're going to Stillwater." He said. "Have you been there?"

"Yes, many years ago."

"With your husband?"

"No, with my daughters." Deb shared. We came here for a weekend on a fishing trip."

"A fishing trip with your daughters? I thought you didn't like fishing that much."

"No, no, you're thinking of men's fishing trips. This is different. The guys went fishing for fish every year. We decided it was time for us to go fishing for fun, fellowship, whatever and we came here to the city to go shopping and to the theater. The Mall of America was just new. We had a great time!"

"Did you ride the river-boat when you were here?"

"Yes, would it still be running this late?"

"On weekends so we can ride it if it is."

As he drove along, Deb felt fatigue coming on. "Mini-nap time, Four AM was a long time ago." She yawned.

"What?" Glen looked puzzled.

"Sometimes I need a Grandma's Power Nap. That's what my grand-kids call them. I need one right now. I have to rejuvenate so excuse me for five minutes." She reclined the seat and leaned back.

"Here," Glen put his arm around her shoulder and pulled her toward him. "Lean here. Five minutes is all?" He asked into her hair.

"Mm huh," she answered and faded. When she woke, she felt his closeness before stirring. She hugged him, then sat up. "Thank you, all better now."

"Does that work?"

"Yes, without it, I stay tired, get ugly. Sorry."

"Don't be. I've never seen anyone do that before." He grinned.

"Get ugly or take a mini-nap?" She laughed.

"The nap bit." He nudged her.

Stillwater was decked in fall colors. They decided to take the river boat to see the trees along the banks. Sitting on the sunny side of the paddlewheel boat with a spiked coffee kept them warm. There weren't many tourists around so it was quiet and relaxing. Juno's restaurant was on the second floor of an old building with a lot of antique memorabilia everywhere. They had lunch, sitting in front of a window that looked over the river and gave a panoramic view of trees of every color. Then they walked Main Street through all of the antique shops. Deb bought a milk-glass honey jar. Glen offered to pay for it but let it go when Deb said she wanted to.

The trolley tour of town was loading as they came back toward the train station, so they suddenly decided to ride it too. Sitting in the last row, they made up their own version of the people who lived in the historic houses the driver was pointing out. They laughed a lot at their own versions. Getting off the trolley, they each tipped the driver. He thanked them and asked if they were celebrating an anniversary or honeymoon.

Glen said "yes". The driver said he could always tell because they seemed so happy. Arm in arm they walked away. It didn't matter, they were celebrating "life".

Glen said it was time to go back to the city. There were other things to do. He took Deb to a Minnesota Wild Pro Hockey game. It was great!. "How did you know I love hockey?" Deb asked.

"I listen." He said. She was constantly impressed by this man. Supper was hot dogs and popcorn and sharing a huge beer. Fall chill was in the air when the game got out so they went back to Glen's for a nightcap. "Start a fire in the fireplace while I get something hot for us." He gestured toward the living room.

"Oh sure, where is the wood?" She asked, and then saw it was gas.

"Like this." He said and pushed a button. The flame appeared immediately. He brushed her cheek with his hand, went to the kitchen and came back with two mugs of cappuccino. From somewhere, music surrounded them. He sat beside her on the sofa and slipped his shoes off. Then he reached down and pulled off Deb's too. "How are your feet? Do you need them rubbed?"

"My feet always need to be rubbed. I love it." She confessed. As he began to rub them. "You know, feet are very sensitive and sensuous. There are lots of nerves in feet. Reflex ology therapy teaches that all pains and ailments can be treated by massaging certain areas of the feet."

"Is that true?" He peered at the foot he rubbed. "You know all of these things about love and feet and stuff."

"I just read about it. I do know what it does to me."

"What does it do to you?" He continued to rub.

"It makes me crazy and I attack!" She lunged at him, taking him by surprise and they fell over on the sofa together.

"Debra!" He sounded stern and then laughed and they lay in each other's arms. "I think I'll do it again."

"Tonight?" She teased.

"I don't dare. I might not be able to control you." He laughed, sitting up. He still held her close. "Or me." He added. "I could get into trouble like this." Then he grabbed two pillows from the end of the sofa and laid them on the coffee table. He put her feet on one and his feet next to them on the same one. Laughing, she adored him more. Sitting in silence and sipped their drinks, they watched the fire. "Ms. Sullivan, this was a special day for me, thanks." He slipped his arm around her. The warmth wasn't just from the fire or the hot drink. Deb dozed. "Tired?"He asked.

"Yes, it has been a wonderful day, but I am tired. If I don't go, I'll be too tired to leave. Will you take me to the motel now?"

"Mm huh, but I don't want to." He kissed her and pushed her away, then he reached for their shoes. He put Deb's shoes on first. She swelled with emotion. It was such a special gesture.

Deb offered to just get out at the door of the motel but he insisted on taking her to her room. "Come in and say good night and then get out of here." She pulled him inside and shut the door. They embraced and kissed making her knees like rubber again. She felt like a teenager having her first kiss. She needed to lean on him to stand. "Glen, I need to have you go. Come in the morning whenever you get ready. I'll be up early. Now, good night."

"What is it with you?" When I start to get romantic with you, you want me to leave. Is there a problem here?" He grinned.

"You don't get it? That is the problem. I could easily drag you to that bed and have you, all of you, now go!"

He stepped back and looked at her. "How you talk! Good night, dear." She locked the door behind him.

☙ CHAPTER 20 ☙

DEB TOOK TIME FOR DEVOTIONS AND reading before Glen showed up in the morning. Opening the door for him, he stepped inside and hugged her. "I've been up for an hour but didn't dare come too early. Hungry?" He asked as he held onto her.

"Yes." She was hungry all right, not necessarily for food, but she didn't tell him. Breakfast was at the Panecuken House where they serve wonderful German pancakes and sausages. Then they visited a flea market and auction sale. Glen said he liked them and Deb did too. They talked about what items they liked and stayed long enough to see what some sold for but they didn't buy anything.

Back at Glen's they went for a walk. Up one path was the large building Deb had seen from the second-floor deck. It was the complex's gym and swimming pool. Glen showed her inside. Several people were swimming and using the gym equipment. He introduced Deb as his "friend." Their reactions were friendly.

Deb took Glen's arm as they walked along the lakeshore path that eventually wandered through the trees. Deb stopped to pick up some leaves. "Minnesota leaves are so much bigger than North Dakota ones."

"Really?" Glen acted amazed.

"Yes, look." She started to show them to him.

He picked up a bunch as if to inspect them but sprinkled them over her head. "Here, have some more."

So Deb scooped up some and threw them at him. "Glen, it's true, now stop." He threw some more at her. A scuffle ensued and she hurried to a bench near the beach and sat down. "Base! Time out!" She laughed.

He ran after her."Coward!" He said as he plopped close by. Then they sat and watched the lake in silence. Glen announced to her."We have a dinner date so let me change and take you back to your motel. You do have dress-up clothes? He asked. Deb waited while Glen got dressed in a gray suit with an orchid shirt and tie, pretty sharp.

At the motel, he read the tourist magazine in the room waiting for her to get ready. Deb had packed a black basic dress with a beaded jacket for dress up. She'd have to wear the same dress for church tomorrow. She had a plain jacket for that. Glen said she looked beautiful in black. He suggested she bring her swimsuit so they could use the hot tub when they came back. She took it in her bag.

Driving south on the freeway, he asked, "Have you ever been to Chanhassen Dinner Theater?"

"Yes, it's great. What's playing?"

"It's a surprise." They were seated in a large curved booth. They both sat at the back facing the stage. The wait person brought them a drink as they poured over the menu. Glen looked up and said. "Oh, oh, my friends are here and they'll be over here when they see us."

"Is that bad?"

"No." He smiled. "Not at all." No sooner said than a couple came toward their table. They sat one on each side after Glen introduced them to Deb. They told her that they wanted to make it a double date tonight but Glen was selfish and wanted be alone with "that woman." They all laughed. Fran, the wife told Deb that Glen would not get away with it next time. Walt said they understood though and were happy that Glen found a woman he wanted to be selfish about. He told Glen he approved of "that woman.". The waiter brought salads for Deb and Glen so Fran and Walt went back to their table saying they were glad to be the first to meet Deb.

"So, what do they know about me, us?"

"They've been good friends since I moved back here. You'll see them again at brunch tomorrow. They know I like you enough to have you come here for a weekend and knowing me and my experience or lack of it, they think I'm serious. All of my friends are concerned about me being the 'single one' in the crowd. They have all tried for years to pair me with women."

"Oh, really! How did that go?" Deb teased.

"It didn't. The last year or so they just gave up and let me be a fifth wheel. Actually, they have made me go along when they do something like an outing or trip. So you can see how they are excited for me when I find a woman I want to be with. They are sort of like my family."

"So, is there pressure for me to live up to some expectation?"

"You will exceed any expectations, no problem. But believe me, and get this straight, I really don't care what they think. I only care about what WE think. They know that I came to see you and you came to see me. They think that is serious. At least it's farther than I've ever gone in a relationship with a woman since they've known me. What they think is important to me because they are my friends but I really only care about us."

"Thank you, Glen. I love that you said it that way." Deb almost said *I love you.* And wondered why she didn't.

The production was <u>*West Side Story*</u>. Deb found herself crying in several scenes. Glen sat close and held her hand as if to comfort her. He shared his handkerchief the first time and then he said she'd have to use her own when he was touched in the place where Tony lay dying.

On the drive home, Glen told her more about his friends that she would meet the next day. "We go to brunch after church so you will meet them then. These are the closest friends I have. One couple is a pastor at the church and his wife. Two of them are people I work with and the others are from the church.

❧ CHAPTER 21 ❧

AT THE HOUSE, GLEN TOOK DEB'S hand and led her to his room. He helped her remove her jacket and threw it on the bed. Pointing to the bathroom, he said, "You first." She took her swimsuit with her and shut the door. When she came out, soft music was playing from the bedroom. Glen was already in the hot tub.

Walking over to the edge, she asked "What's going on?"

"I wanted you to do this with me but thought you might say no."

"I still might." She still stood on the outside with a towel on her shoulders. "Why would I say no?"

"You told me you didn't invite me into your hot tub because it was intimate. I hoped by now we could be that intimate," he argued.

Deb slipped the towel off and climbed into the water. "Well, I usually hot tub alone so I dress scantily. That makes it intimate."

"Oh, you mean you don't wear much, if anything." He caught on.

"Well, I am alone.." She tried to explain.

"Yes. Now I see. He grinned. "Well, we don't have to be intimate like that least not now. So are you ok with this?" Deb got in. They sat across from each other touching legs.

"Yes, this is acceptable." Deb agreed. He began to rub Deb's feet. "That's cheating! You already know what that does to me." She warned.

"Mm huh." He lifted her foot to his lips. She slid slowly off the seat until she started to go under the water on purpose.

"Deb…" Glen grabbed her and pulled her up. Deb started to giggle and they were wrapped in each other's arms and legs. The feeling inside was wonderful, almost painful. "Deb," he groaned, "get away from me before it's too late. Maybe this wasn't a good idea."

She sat up away from him. "It was a wonderful idea, we can handle it."

He reminded her. "We haven't talked as much about 'us' as we promised we would, have we? And we need to."

"Yes, you're right. So what is happening to us?"

"Deb, I'm in love with you." He choked up and his voice faded. "I know that."

"Glen, I'm in love with you. I don't know what to do about it but I really didn't want to love again. I wanted to be alone. I have to share something about that, Glen."

"Me too, Deb. I need to tell you about my fears. Honest to God, I swore I would never marry again, not after what I went through with Myrna."

"What you went through? What do you mean? Her illness?"

"Her cancer, her dying and something else. The last six months with her were sheer agony. It got so she was not herself. She was someone else, lying there, just taking up space and room I was more obsessed with what I was going through than caring about her. She seemed a lost cause. She was going to die anyway, why not now and get it over with. This frail, ugly skeleton of a person was not my wife anymore. I didn't feel like her husband either. It changed me forever. I wanted to get away from the whole scene and at the same time I felt guilty if I wasn't with her. Toward the end, Myrna didn't want to be alone but would just lie there and not even respond though you knew she was awake. My compassion for her just wasn't enough anymore. I wanted to scream. I felt sorry for myself. Why me? Then the guilt would set in and I was ashamed of myself. I wasn't having the pain. The tubes and dressings were attached to her. How could I pity myself? How could I be so selfish? I wasn't going to be dead when it was over but it seemed I wouldn't survive either. I prayed for more love and compassion, enough to get us through it all."

Deb just let him pour it out. At times his lip quivered and he'd stop for a bit. "You know the people who kill their loved ones in mercy killings? I understand that after what I went through. I could have easily helped Myrna do it as much for her as for me. I was so selfish. I never want to go through that again."

They were both quiet for a few minutes." Glen, only you know..." She tried to give him time.

"No, let me finish. I still think I believe that. I would swear love of any kind just isn't worth it. Now that I've met you, it's like I forgot my resolve. You have that effect on me." He chuckled and squeezed her hand. "Here I am being selfish again. I only think of myself and my needs. I love you and want to spend the rest of my life with you. I ignore what life might hold for us. Getting old and decrepit and having aches and pains is forgotten. And I know they will come, cripes I have some of them now.

I even bargain with myself that I'll take care of you if that is what it comes to someday. I'll have you any way you want, however it's possible. I want you permanently, married or not."

They were sitting on opposite sides of the hot tub not touching.

"I'm not the man I used to be. I cry more and I laugh easier. I have more compassion for others. But I have never loved since then so I'm not sure if I can again. It scares me."

"Glen, no one knows what a loved one goes through just watching and waiting for them to die, especially when they suffer. Anyone who hasn't gone through it doesn't know. You do." She tried to reason with him. "Don't be so hard on yourself. You are human. I would be surprised if it didn't change you, Glen. You would be a person without heart if it didn't. You can't be the same person you were before that. It isn't possible." There was silence again.

He spoke first. "Deb, I still have to tell you another thing."

"I haven't had my turn." Deb raised his hand to her lips, then looked at his hand. " You are getting wrinkled skin."

"Old age." He shrugged and grinned. Her heart hurt for him.

"Time to get out." Deb stood up. "Chapter two coming up." Glen got out and helped her. The strap of her suit dropped off her shoulder. He touched it, started to slide it down instead of up. He put his fingers under her other strap and slid it down too. Deb couldn't stop him. They both froze for what seemed like a long time. Then with a groan he shoved them both up. Deb wrapped her arms around his waist and crushed him close. He hugged her back, then grabbed her arms and held her tight before letting go of her.

"I'll get dressed. We need to talk some more." He went into the shower room and shut the door. Deb's clothes were in there. She found a large terry robe in his closet, slipped out of the wet suit, and wrapped the robe around her tying it tightly. It touched the floor, it was so long but would have to do. The bedroom was not the place to continue their talk, she decided.

Switching on the fireplace, Deb settled on the sofa, she waited until Glen came. He'd put on sweats. He started to sit by her but changed his mind and sat in his chair. "This is safer." He assured her. "It sounds like we both need to do some talking, begin somewhere in our pasts in order to go on into the future."

"Yes, I think so. Do you want to finish or shall I tell you my story, Glen?"

He raised his hands, palms toward her. "Don't tell me, Deb unless it makes a difference to you. Nothing will make a difference to me."

"Glen, I love you for that but I think I need to tell you this so you know where I am in my life so you don't misunderstand some things that may affect our relationship. Like your experience with Myrna, I am changed by the last forty years."

Taking a deep breath she began, "when I married Dan, I became part of him. My goals, hopes, dreams were all wrapped up in him, for him. We were he. I was he. I not only didn't have 'me', but really didn't feel even like a 'we'. I was Mrs. Sullivan, Dr. Sullivan's wife, but I was no one unless I was a part of him, even my name. Everyone including Dan thought I should be proud to be Mrs. Dr. Sullivan. I was proud to be his wife and it wouldn't have mattered what profession he chose, I wasn't as thrilled with the medical profession as he was. It's just that there was never a time when he was my husband. We were always identified by him. Even our kids were Dr. Sullivan's Kids. We were never our own people. The kids resented it as they grew up and I knew why they felt that way.

"Dan was in medical school when we met and married. The years changed me. At first, I didn't notice it. I was busy with house and home. I worked until we had a baby and then I took in sewing and babysat. His life was totally wrapped up in medicine. I, we got what was left. Sometimes, he used up all of his 'nices' elsewhere. He loved me. As much as he was capable of loving anyone besides himself. We had passion to spare when there was time for us. Then the kids started coming. We had three in four years. By the time Dan finished residency, we had all four of them. We were as poor as church mice for many years. I didn't mind, I was so busy with my babies and health problems from having kids in such a hurry that I didn't seem to have other needs. Dan was never home. When he was, he slept. Our kids didn't know who he was. I expected all of that then. Besides, I adored him but it never changed."

Deb stopped and shivered and pulled Glen's robe closer round her. How much should she share? "Ah." She tried again.

"Would it help if I held your hand?" Glen offered. She started to cry. He got up and took her hand, pulling her up. He pulled the robe tightly around her and tightened the tie. He led her to his big recliner pulling her down sort of beside him. Deb felt so protected and safe. She cried again. He said not a word.

God, how I love him at this moment. She started again. "I did all the wifely things and was as perfect a doctor's wife as I could be. I was a gracious hostess and a supportive helpmate. I gave receptions and hosted parties for hundreds at a time. I sat with patients whose spouses were dying or having a baby or took care of their children when they were sick. I was involved in volunteer work and charity to support the community. You could call me the super mom, always involved with my kid's activities and events.

I loved what I did. It was my goal to be the best I could especially as a mother. In spite of all of that, Dan came first I believed that was the way it was supposed to be. That was what my wedding vows said to me. I believed it so there was the way my life would be. That is even what my church, faith taught me.

Dan was a good provider, financially. He insisted he gave

me all I needed, everything I asked. He constantly told me that everything 'we' had was 'ours'. But it wasn't really. Everything we had was ours as long as he had control. He just bought me something when he wanted me to feel loved. Even then, he was in control of whatever he bought. He never got it. Besides that, he constantly had to be assured of his worth. He thought his value was in what he did, how much he made, how many committees he was on and titles he had. He was a workaholic. The world loves and admires them. Their reward isn't just the money though that is a barometer of their success. They just never have enough, not money or power or attention and they are willing to work themselves to death to have it.

Five years ago, he had decided to look for another position. He was getting tired of family practice. He had several job offers in Grand Island. He said he was ready to slow down in his practice.

I told him I was moving to Grand Island and that staying in Mallory was not an option for me. He couldn't think of anything but his own needs for recognition and attention and his love of medicine. I told him he would have to do what he thought best for his future, immediate and long-term. I had to do the same. He never once asked me to stay. He admitted a year later that he thought I would get my 'need to do my own thing' out of my system and come back. He never got it. Yet, I don't think he ever thought we would divorce. He thought we'd be 'happily married' forever no matter how distant or disconnected we were. He always took me for granted as if I would always be there to take care of him. I was his gofer and I was supposed to stand beneath his pedestal and worship him like everyone else did.

The first years of our marriage I complied because I loved him. The day came when I didn't do it out of love but obligation. He always expected from me but seldom did either of us expect anything from him. It was my fault too that I never asked, never expected until it was too late.

Love like that is like a plant that is watered but never nourished, eventually it dies. And mine did. I can't believe his love for me remained. By the time I moved to Grand Island my thinking was that I deserved it. I was too old and had no alternative, anyway. It was a habit, a way of life. The knowns were less risky than the unknowns. I respected Dan as a good doctor, but that is not what a marriage is. I was settling for less than I deserved.

Many of my friends were like me. One word described our marriages, 'resignation'. We called it marriage but it was like two ships passing in the night. Dan wanted to leave it the way it was. It was ok with him. He said he loved me. His kind of love wasn't enough. It wasn't the kind of love that would keep me with him for the next twenty years. I'd rather be really alone."

"I was living a lie, Glen. I felt like a hypocrite putting on the front in public but in private, he went his way and I mine. I was alone but I can't say I was lonely. I had family and friends. I had my job and more hobbies and projects than I would ever get done. I wasn't bored or sad or unhappy. But I wasn't fulfilled and wouldn't be until I said good bye to that marriage.

There is a saying, 'Insanity is doing the same things over and over and expecting different results'."

Deb shifted next to Glen. His arms held her tenderly. "I'm telling you this Glen, because I never want to live that way again. I want more. I want to give more or just stay as I am. Glen, you need to know I had filed for divorce just before Dan had his final heart attack. If he hadn't died, I would have gone through with it."

"Did Dan know you wanted a divorce?" Glen interrupted her story.

"Yes, I told him that I had seen a lawyer and was going to file for divorce two days before." She choked. "Before he took sick."

"Do you blame your news for his death?"

"No, not now. I suppose I did at first but few people knew about it. There was one last front to put on until after the funeral. I had the grief and pain of having loved him all those years and never really getting through to him and now I never would. My grief was real, I grieved a relationship that was long dead. I had the unfinished business of divorce that it seemed would never end the pain. It took a long time to sort it all out. I finally found peace with it all. Now, it's been a couple of years and I love my life alone… or did until now." Turning to Glen accusingly.

"And then I came along." He finished.

"Yes, you came along." She kissed his cheek. "This is the last thing I need to tell you. All the rest of it I could have left out but it puts you where you are in my life. Because of you, being alone isn't such a precious thing."

"Do you mean that?"

"Yes, if I left here and never saw you again, I would be lonely now. You gave me a taste of what togetherness can be with someone you love." He held her close breathing into her hair. She could feel his heartbeat against her back. She finally relaxed but feeling spent. There was just silence now.

After a few minutes, Glen shifted and spoke. "Deb, the other thing I wanted to share with you. It's important too, especially after what you just shared. I have to finish what I started to say in the hot tub about Myrna and me. I loved her. There were many wonderful things about her. She was a good wife and we both worked at our marriage yet, it wasn't romantic love. I thought the reason was because I was older and she had been married and there were three kids in the house. Kids alone can dampen passion."

"Do I know?" Deb agreed.

"All of that gave me reason for my lack of passion. Deb, I don't know if this will make a difference to you but I need to tell you this because it does to me and is a measure of how I feel about you." He hesitated.

He held her hand. "Now, I want to, I need to say this to you. Deb, I never forgot you. I know that sounds silly, the little we ever saw of each other thirty some years ago. But I always compared women with you. It even seemed stupid to me. I didn't know you that well and had no reason to think you would live up to my thoughts or fantasies of you. I just believed you were the kind of woman I wanted to love and used that as my gauge.

Myrna was the closest I came to that. I told myself it was

my chance at happiness in marriage. Being with you was not a possibility. I thought it was sick and stupid of me but I couldn't help it. Deb, the way I love you right now, I never felt for Myrna. In fact, it probably came between us. She was not you. I kept a dream that is now coming true. I can't believe it but I love you so much, it hurts." He stopped and reached for a tissue. He was crying. "I love you." He choked and wiped his eyes.

"Glen, it has been a lot of years since I was in love at all so I can only tell you that I don't ever remember loving Dan like I love you."

"So what are we going to do about this situation?" He asked.

"Glen, I can't promise you that I won't get sick and have to have someone to care for me. It could be the other way around. Can our love for each other be enough to overcome that?"

"We can't know, we can only live it."

"Right."

"Will you be happy having me around all of the time when you love your independence and aloneness so much? If I'm going to marry you or live with you, I want us to share our time and activities. There are things I will want to do that you won't and I can respect that but if we don't have the same interests, we will still be alone. I've been alone for too many years. Deb, I am probably more ready for companionship than you are. What if I get in your way? Will what I can offer you rob you of your privacy?"

"I don't know. What can you offer me?" She asked.

He was more serious. "Well, I'll try to give you everything you want." Glen looked at her and added. "What do you want? Maybe I can't."

"I want…." She started. "Maybe I need to tell you what I don't want. I don't want possessions and things. I have enough of them. I don't want money. I have enough to be comfortable yet not extravagant.

Glen, I want compassion, conversation, companionship, fun, love, lovemaking, sex, passion, warmth, caring, and… and I want to give all of that to you."

He shifted in his chair with an amused look on his face. "Whoa, I'm not sure I can give you all of that. Do you think I can?"

"You could try. I could try. I'm willing to take a chance. We could enjoy trying together."

Their emotions were overwhelmed now. Deb reached her arms around him. They sat quietly in each other's arms. "I don't want you to leave me tonight." He whispered to her, "ever."

"I don't want to but I have to for now."

Both of them were exhausted by their emotional conversation. The silence, Glen's big chair was comforting and peaceful. Deb looked down as he shifted beside her. His robe was falling open. "I need to get up. I need to go."

"I don't want you to leave me, Deb. Don't go to the motel tonight." He noticed and carefully pulled the robe together at the neck. "Stay here with me." he pleaded.

"Glen…" She started to protest.

"Just stay here. I don't want to let you go tonight or any

night." He pulled the front of the robe together better and tightened the belt. "I'll behave, honest."

Getting up Deb faced him. "Ok, I'll stay. You don't have another bed. Give me one of your shirts, a pillow and blanket. I'll sleep here on the sofa."

Glen got up too. "Deal." He shook her hand, then put his arm firmly around her shoulder, walking to the bedroom. He stepped into the closet and stuck his head out. "Any particular color you prefer?"

Deb laughed, "Whatever colors you think I look good in, pink, blue."

He brought a blue plaid flannel shirt out. "This do? My pink ones are dirty."

"It's me!" She went into the bathroom, gathered her clothes and put the shirt on with the robe over it. "One more thing."

Glen had a blanket and pillow in his arms. "What now?" He tried to sound stern.

"A pair of socks," Deb sat on the edge of the bed. "My feet get cold."

"Socks! Any particular color, do you want them to match your nightie?" He teased. He opened a drawer and grabbed a pair, seated her on the bed and knelt in front of her. "They'll go over your knees." He grinned up at her and took her foot. "It is cold." He held it for a moment and then put on one and then the other, pulling them up her leg. Then he grinned up at her. Deb's heart melted.

She reached out and pulled him to her. "Glen, I love you. We need to talk more but not tonight, tomorrow."

"Yeah, we need to get some sleep. Separately, I know. Now, get out of here." He pointed to the door.

Deb took the blanket and pillow then turned at the door, "Good night, then."

Glen kissed her softly. "Good night."

⚔ CHAPTER 22 ⚔

GEN LAY IN HIS HUGE BED alone. He didn't remember it being so big and empty before. He always seemed to fill the length but hadn't noticed there was lots of space around him. *Tomorrow, maybe we can talk about filling this bed with her.* He was exhausted so he slept peacefully.

Deb shut off the light and the fireplace, stretched out on the sofa and covered herself. She felt content and safe.

It seemed no time until she woke with pale light coming through the curtain. Her watch read seven o'clock. "*I don't remember what time church is, better get up.* She went into the utility bathroom, then down the hallway to Glen's room. The door was ajar so she pushed it open enough to step in. Glen lay still. He seemed to be sleeping. Then he began to snore, louder and louder.

"Oh, no, not that."

Suddenly, he reared up with one giant snort.

"You nut!" Deb jumped on the bed and grabbed him by the shoulders. He pulled her down and they lay laughing. "What time is church?"

"We'll go to ten o'clock worship service, ok?"

"I've got to get going. May I use the bathroom upstairs? I can't go back to the motel like this."

"Sure, there are towels and stuff up there. Let me know if you need anything else like having your back washed."

Throwing him a grin, Deb gathered her clothes and went upstairs to get as ready as she could. Glen was at the front door getting the newspaper when Deb looked over the balcony. He was dressed and ready. He looked up and smiled. "Ready?"

"Hi! No, not really," peering over the balcony. Coming down the stairs, "this is so neat!" In front of Glen, she said. "I have to finish at the motel."

"I'll take you over there now if you wish. Or you can take the car and come back. Why don't you just check out and stay with the same accommodations you had last night?"

"Yeah, might as well. Glen, I need a glass of juice." In the kitchen he kissed her. "Ewe, I need to brush my teeth, that must have tasted awful." Deb made a face.

"Didn't notice, I'd kiss you under any condition." He had set some food on the bar. "Anything else? We're having brunch after church. How about a muffin or fruit for now?"

"Something, anything." Sharing the comics, they sat at the bar. Checking her watch, "Glen, I've got to go. Come with me and read the newspaper while I get ready and packed."

Glen belonged to Central Lutheran downtown, a huge older church with stone and brick on the outside and stone with dark ornate wood on the inside. The sanctuary would hold six to eight hundred people and there were lofts on three sides facing the altar.

A pastor in a white alb and vestments was greeting arriving worshipers. He made his way to them, smiling broadly. "Glen!" He said reaching out his hand. "And you are..." he turned to Deb and took her hand.

Glen spoke "Pastor Dave, this is Deb, Debra Sullivan."

"So nice to meet you, Ms. Sullivan I've heard a lot about you."

"You may call me Deb, May I call you Pastor Dave?"

"Please do. Everyone else does."

" Thank you, I'm glad to meet you too."

"We'll talk more at brunch I need to find out if all I heard is really true." He teased.

Other friends came over too. Deb would never remember all of their names but they were welcoming to her. Glen steered her into the enormous sanctuary as the pipe organ pealed a hymn, they took their seats in a pew near the front. The worship was quite formal and reverent. They shared a hymnal again, touching hands underneath. He'd touch Deb's fingers distracting her. She tried to act "normal" but felt like everyone must notice the way they felt about each other. The truth is, they probably didn't notice or care.

After church, the brunch crowd walked to a hotel a block away. In the dining room, a large table had been reserved for twelve near the back for Glen and his friends. The pastor and his wife, Sharon and the couple that Deb had met at the theater were there. The other church friends were kind enough to repeat their names. It was a friendly, laughing group. Champagne, coffee and juice were served and it was taken for granted that everyone would have the buffet. But no one got up. The pastor prayed a blessing and everyone lifted their champagne glass for a toast. They toasted friendship and fellowship and Glen and his "new friend", Deb in particular, that she would be their friend too. She felt so welcome.

Finally the crowd got up for food and visited while waiting in line. Deb was starved by then. She felt a bit tipsy after alcohol on a near-empty stomach. Glen stood behind her with his hand on her waist. He noticed. "Are you ok?" He whispered.

"Yes, I just need some food."

"Cheap drunk," Glen accused her, tightening his grip on her waist. She giggled again. With plates piled high, the group fell quiet, but as dessert came, they began to ask questions. How did Glen and Deb meet? When? They were pressing for answers. Deb turned to Glen "They're your friends, you tell them," Deb urged him.

He took her hand."Help me." Everyone laughed.

"I didn't just meet Deb a month or so ago, you know. We've known each other for over thirty years."

"Boy, are they slow." Bill cut in, more laughter.

"Now, let me tell it." He insisted. "When we met before, Deb was married but I wasn't. I was teaching school and my brother was teaching and coaching in the town where she lived. I met her at a party at my brother's house. I didn't... I wanted to..." He turned to Deb. "You tell them this part." The group was calling for answers.

"Well, without going into detail, Glen didn't know I was married so he planned to call me for a date. He asked a friend what my number was because he didn't know my last name.

He told the lady his intentions, and she told him he could call me but my husband and kids might not like it." Everyone laughed.

Glen continued. "So I was a gentleman and stayed out of her life."He looked at Deb and added. "Almost."

More laughter "Whoa," they chimed in.

"Well, we both went to a wedding of a mutual friend's son. Deb's husband went fishing instead. Nothing happened that I could brag about." He hesitated, "or be ashamed of. We were just there. Though I was attracted to her, I didn't let on. Then we only saw each other one or two other times after that, right?" Glen looked at Deb.

"Yes, I guess except that everyone knew you liked me because you wanted to ask me for a date and you called the town crier to ask what my last name was. It was like taking an ad in the newspaper."

"Oh yeah, that's true." Glen agreed, looking guilty. "She remembers that stuff better than I do."

Deb added. "It's hard to be nostalgic when you can't remember anything!" The whole crowd laughed.

"Did you know he wanted to date you?" Sharon asked.

"Yes, the news got out. There were lots of friends on the wedding trip. We had chaperones."

Deb could feel herself getting warm. How far into details do I need to go to satisfy them she wondered. Looking at Glen to rescue her. "Then we met again a month ago and we are both single now so," she hesitated. "I quit." That was all she was going to volunteer.

Pastor Dave spoke now. "Deb, until now we know you only

from what Glen has told us. Tell us about you so we may know you better."

Bless him for changing the subject. "Thank you," she said to him. Then, "Well, I was married to a family physician for forty years. I have four children and seven grandchildren. I am active in a lay ministry program and am a certified chaplain. I work for my church as a visitation chaplain. I also have done some pulpit supply and public speaking."

Pastor Dave spoke again. "Boy, could we use you here in our parish!" Others voiced agreement.

Glen added. "She's a good preacher. She has already been preaching to me."

The men especially laughed. Deb poked him and just said. "Glen!"

"She's a grandma, a preacher chaplain-lady with a sense of humor and she's beautiful. Great! huh!" The friends clapped.

"So what about the two of you now?" June Kelvin asked. "You haven't told us how you met again after thirty years and a marriage each."

Someone else chimed in, he told me."

"Me too." Someone else said.

"Well!" Came from another.

"And how serious is this second time around?" One friend asked.

Glen squeezed her hand. "I went to Grand Island to sign the papers selling the last of my family's farm. I heard some time before from my sister-in-law that Deb's husband had died a year or so ago. I decided to call her while I was there. I thought we'd meet for coffee and we did. We went out a few more times that weekend. Now she's here visiting me. We like each other, ok?"

"Like, love, what…" they wanted more details.

Smiling at each other, Deb looked at their faces. They weren't just snooping or nosy. They really cared about Glen. He is family and they love him. Glen put his arm around Deb and whispered in her ear. "May I tell them more, I mean about us?"

"Whatever you're comfortable with." She said, feeling a blush but had no idea where he was going with this.

Glen turned to Greg Summers next to him. "Pour a little champagne for everyone. This may call for a toast." Everyone caught on. Glasses clinked and champagne flowed. Then Glen turned his chair and his long legs toward Deb. "Ready?" He reached in his pocket and pulled out a small package. She felt like she couldn't breathe. "This is a surprise for Deb too." Glen announced, "ahem. I may have been slow the first thirty years I knew you but I'm in a hurry now. You won't get away from me this time. I have a gift for you and I want to give it to you now, I think."

Laughter erupted. "In front of all these people, friends of mine and I hope they are yours too. If they weren't friends that I trust, I wouldn't do this." Not only were the people at our table watching but the entire dining room was, including the help. He took Deb's hand and put the box in it.

"This is for you because I love you." He blushed. Everyone clapped and cheered.

She took off the ribbon and opened the box. There was a set of three rings in the box. Two were bands with tiny diamonds in rows. The third was a huge diamond with the small rows fitted around it. They were breathtaking. "Glen!" Was all she could say. She began to cry. The friends cooed and clapped. He helped her stand up. They hugged and kissed forgetting there was a roomful of people watching. Glen wiped her tears. "I love you," She whispered in his ear.

The box of rings was passed around. There were toasts to Deb and Glen. And more questions about their plans. When the rings came back, Glen put the diamond on Deb. It fit perfectly. "The others are for later," he said, putting the box back in his pocket.

It was Glen's and Deb's turn to toast "to his old friends and Deb's new ones. They are one and the same now. The couple gave the crowd of friends assurance that they would be informed of their plans when they were definite. It would just be soon. Glen said by the end of the year. He was reminded that it wasn't long 'til the end of the year. "When you find the love of your life at this age." Glen answered. "You don't want to waste days let alone years."

Leaving with hugs and well wishes from everyone, they felt such support. Their friends promised to help celebrate when the time came.

Deb marveled how he got the rings. "I was always with you. When did you get them, not this weekend?"

"Yes, I got them today in church. You just have to know the right people. I have a good friend who owns a jewelry store. I called him and told him what I wanted and he slipped them to me when I hung up our coats before church."

"You are amazing. Are you sure you didn't get them before?"

"Honest! That would have been egotistical and presumptuous of me to have gotten them before you admitted you loved me." He smiled.

"Yes, yes it would." Deb grinned and poked him.

"Do you really like them? Is it the kind of design you like? They are really only symbolic and we can go to the store today and exchange them for what you would like. I will confess that I stopped into my friend's store and looked at rings he had last week. I just mentioned the ones I liked and hoped you would. I only guessed your size. It was just a guess."

"You guessed perfectly." She admired her ring. "It is exactly what I would have chosen. The other two rings too. I'm simply amazed that you knew. It is not a coincidence, you know. I don't believe in coincidences. They are what we call miracles when we don't have another explanation." Deb leaned over and kissed his cheek. "Thank you, I love you, not just for the rings but for you."

"I hope so. I love you too." They held hands.

✦ CHAPTER 23 ✦

BACK AT HIS HOUSE, WITH PAPER and pencil, the afternoon was spent writing options, possible problems, things like jobs and retirement, cars and campers, houses and furniture. Combining stuff and eliminating duplicates had to be decided. They wrote it all down so they wouldn't have to go over it again or guess what they had decided already. Glen didn't have lots of furnishing and agreed his house needed a feminine touch.

Wedding dates and times to meet each other's kids made them realize time was short. They called Deb's sons, Jay and Dan, Jr. in Fargo and made a date to meet with them there in two weeks. "Then I'll have an excuse to see you sooner." Glenn gazed at her.

Carol, Deb's daughter in Omaha and her family were delighted when they called and invited themselves for Thanksgiving. Glen's stepdaughter, Tami living in the Twin City Area so they called her. Glen told her about Deb then the women talked for about ten minutes. Tami was thrilled that Glen would have someone in his life again. They set a time on Monday morning after Thanksgiving to meet for breakfast. Tami chose a restaurant close to the airport for Deb's convenience. Glen took the phone and told her when they hoped to have their wedding. And that their family would be welcome. She said they would like to. Glen was pleased that she was anxious to meet Deb.

Then they called the two stepsons who live out east. Glen talked for a while to each of them and then he introduced Deb over the phone. Glen said Deb owns a camper and they hope to travel east in spring or summer. He promised to see them when they did. Glen's stepsons, Bob and Phil were happy for Glen and said they looked forward to meeting Deb.

Business was discussed all afternoon. Since Glen didn't have the extra furnishings it would take to do the rooms upstairs, Deb's things would fit well. She also planned to give keepsakes and other things the kids wanted to her children when they came for Christmas. Whatever didn't make the lists would be sold at auction. Glen admitted that his house needed the addition of her things. They decided to keep Deb's camper in case they wanted to use it next summer and see how they liked camping together. Glen had never done much camping but Deb had.

They wanted to be married in Deb's church in Grand Island, a "family members only" service and then a reception or dinner or wedding dance for everyone else. Details would be worked out. Later they'd have a celebration with friends in the city though Glen was sure they would make every effort to come to Grand Island, even if it would be winter.

At the airport, Deb and Glen waited for the plane to take Deb back to Grand Island, back to her privacy, her aloneness and now because of him, her loneliness. Back to a place she loves but not enough to take the place of love for this man. Holding hands, they savored the moments left. When the security line diminished, it was time for her to go. Glen walked her that far. They hugged and kissed. He whispered. "I love you. I miss you already." He had tears in his eyes.

That made Deb cry seeing a big strapping man so emotional. "I'll call you when I get home, ok? It was a wonderful weekend, Glen. Don't spoil it by being sad. I love you." She turned and went toward her gate.

Glen went home alone. He'd been alone for eight years. Perhaps he was too set in his ways by now. He was used to being by himself. At his age he never expected it to be any other way. His life had fallen into a routine that he expected. His work was interesting though he'd thought he'd retire one of these years.

He had good friends who shared their lives with him. What he didn't have was family to go home to or with. There was this pang of aloneness, the empty feeling with no one to say good night or good morning to. That is what being alone is.

Glen thought, *I need to savor every moment of life now that I have someone to share it with. Until now, I never had a timetable. It didn't matter when I retired, now it does. I won't want to go off to work when Deb is home. I can't imagine running out of things to talk about or do with her. I pray she feels the same.*

I will work at being thoughtful enough for Deb to have privacy she needs. She liked that room upstairs with all of the windows and

*the deck. That would make a good room for her sewing and writing
and 'getting away' times.*

*Then I'll turn that storage room into my office as I had planned.
Deb can help me. She's good at decorating and organizing. I'll need
it for an office now. I can do some free lance work at home by computer.
That would be interesting and give me something to do.*

He smiled thinking; *It's amazing, she told me that she not only
dreamed of a house like this for many years but had the plans for one
that she never gave up on building. Now, she would have the man she
loved and that house too. That should make her more willing to give
up her house and property that is amazing there in Grand Island.
She had said it was too much to take care of by herself so this is an
opportune time for her to make a change. This is one she probably
hadn't planned.*

*When she saw that room upstairs, she about swooned. I remember
telling her she could have it. At that time, I wasn't sure I meant it. It is
a perfect room to "do her thing" in. I hope she will make it "hers."*

He drove into the garage, shut the door and went into the
house. It was dark and silent. Though it was only ten o'clock,
he went into his bedroom. He turned on some music and
crawled into bed with his unfinished novel. He'd read until
Deb called.

Deb settled into her seat grateful that no one sat beside
her. With her notebook in her lap, she stared at the lights
outside trying to think of everything she had to do now. As a
list maker, it helped to read the list. *"What am I getting myself
into? Have I had enough time alone since Dan's death? I never felt
lonely until now. Alone is comfortable, lonesome hurts."* She closed
her eyes and tried to visualize life without Glen now.

She told the kids she'd call when she got in but when she called them, they were already at the airport. They each gave her a hug. "How was your weekend, Mom?" Peg wanted to know.

"It was great. We had a wonderful time. I'm tired though."

"But it's a good tired, Mom. You look great."

Peg grabbed her mom's bag and noticed. "What is this?"

"This? Oh, this. Why, it's a ring." Deb joked.

"Mom, it's a ring, A ring! Is there some meaning to it or did you just go shopping for a bauble?"

"It was a gift… from Glen." Her mother confessed.

"It has a meaning?"

"Yes, it means we are getting serious."

"So, when is the wedding? Is it that serious?" Peg questioned.

"Yes, Peg. We're talking of the end of the year if it works out."

"Are you rushing it a bit?"

In the car they continued. "Well, kids, when you are as old as we are, it isn't a rush, it's an urgency."

They laughed but said "Mom, you're not that old." Ron said

"Mom, if this is what you want, I'm happy for you." Peg assured her.

She told them of their plans so far by the time they pulled up to Deb's house.

"Thanks for the ride, kids. I need to call Glen when I get in."

Ron carried her bags into the house, as usual. They all said they loved each other. Deb thanked them for coming and for being her kids.

Deb called Glen and heard his deep voice. "Hi" was all he said.

"You knew it was I?"

"Well, at least I hoped it was. No one else would call me at this hour. Besides, I need to ask you something." Glen sounded so serious. "A question that will change my life and maybe yours temporarily."

"Yes, anything, What?" Deb was curious.

"Would you think I was a nuisance if I called you every night just to make sure you still love me and to tell you I love you and say 'good night'?"

"No, dear, I wouldn't think that, I would love it. Soon you will be expected to say that every morning and night in person so you could just get started now."

Deb gave her official resignation at the church so by the time she met Glen and her sons in Fargo in two weeks, she would be unemployed. The church staff wasn't surprised but they questioned Deb's haste. She admitted some concern at first. But reasoned if they live to be in their eighties, they only have twenty years to make up a lifetime. Deb knew that whatever good years they had left needed to be started soon. She and pastor set the wedding date for Friday Evening, December 30. She told him that she and Glen had decided on a private, family/close friend's ceremony. Then have a reception dinner away from the church. Deb wanted it catered so the women of the congregation wouldn't serve but could be guests. The congregation would be generally invited and announcements sent to out-of-town friends and relatives."

Glen and Deb both enjoy dancing. They had danced at the infamous weekend wedding dance thirty-some years ago, so wanted dancing at the reception. Deb would have to get on it right away before reception sized places were all taken. It was that time of year.

Deb's last weeks of work were emotional. Saying goodbye to her people that she had grown to know and love, she cried with them. They promised to make sure they came to the celebration of Deb's marriage. She told them they would be called before being picked up by a senior's van.

A problem arose though, they all wanted to attend the wedding ceremony. Deb began to rethink the plan and she promised to talk to Glen about it.

✠ CHAPTER 24 ✠

FRIDAY, DEB LEFT FOR FARGO BY mid-morning. It was five hours for her. Glen planned to leave at noon, so they'd arrive about the same time. As she drove, Deb made a list of things to talk to Glen about. She prayed that her boys would be happy for her and would like Glen.

She thought, *how different Glen is from their father. Dan was intense and driven, easily annoyed and excited. Very often, he was angry with those he should care for the most. Glen, in contrast, is relaxed and laid back. He is cautious but loves a new adventure and fun. He's been alone long enough to learn to care for himself, and yet he loved having someone to take care of and care for him. Kind and thoughtful, he appreciates what I do. It has been hard for me to trust his kindness because of my past experience but I'm learning.*

One of my shortcomings with Dan had been that I was independent and stubborn and wanted to appear self- sufficient. He was a workaholic so I became one too. If he could, I could too. I never asked for his help, even when I was sick. I expected him to see my needs, I shouldn't have to ask, he should know. I even distrusted motives if he did show he cared. I prayed I have learned from my past mistakes.

Time passed quickly with her thoughts to occupy her and she was parking at the hotel. Taking her bags, she stepped to the registration desk. Stating her name, Deb Sullivan and that Glen Jarvis had made the reservations, the clerk said yes, her room was ready. Handing Deb a key card she volunteered that Mr. Jarvis had not arrived yet and his room was next to Deb's as he had requested. She smiled and Deb thanked her feeling a glow gathering on her face.

They had pool side rooms connected by a door. Deb set her bag down, hung her garment bag and opened her side of the adjoining door. She stripped to her slip and put on a robe. Then she lay down on the bed covering her feet with the spread and napped.

At his desk at Majestic, Incorporated, Glen thought he'd never get done with last-minute calls. Barb, his secretary set the final file on his desk and said, "this is your last call, Boss." She smiled. "Then you can go play!" Glen grinned and picked up the phone. As he hung up, he grabbed his jacket and briefcase.

"I'm out of here!" He waved.

"Have fun, Boss." Barb called out.

"Meeting future in-laws? Fun!" Glen stopped at a deli drive-through. He bought a sandwich and drink and headed out onto the freeway. Checking the clock in the Buick, it was twelve-thirty. He'd be there in four hours. *I hope Deb gets there first. I've learned patience over a lifetime, but I just don't want to waste time away from her. We never have enough time to talk over the phone it seems. We should have time this weekend.*

Deb's sons planned to meet them in the hotel bar at six-thirty for dinner. Glen knew several good eating places in Fargo, but thought *I'll get my future stepson's advice. Being a diplomat, he hoped would impress them a bit. I also need to tell Deb about possibly coming early or staying late at Thanksgiving time so my friends can have a shower for us. I tried to convince them it wasn't necessary but they insist it is. Since Deb wasn't working now, it shouldn't be a problem.*

He pulled up to the main entrance of the Ramada Inn and spotted Deb's van so he parked beside it. His excitement rose. He had to concentrate on remaining cool while registering. The clerk knew him because he'd stayed here on business but he'd always been alone.

"Mr. Jarvis, good to see you. Your room is ready and Ms. Sullivan has already arrived." Miss Vetter volunteered.

"Thank you." Glen replied. "Bill me for both rooms, please?"

"Certainly, Mr. Jarvis." She smiled, handing him his key card. "Ms. Sullivan is in the adjoining room, as you requested. Enjoy your stay."

He felt his face flush so he quickly turned and grabbed his bag. Obviously, he hadn't "met a woman in a motel room" before and it showed. Actually, they were being respectful by having two rooms. So why should this bother him?

He stepped into his room and saw the adjoining door. He set his bag down and threw his jacket on the bed. He opened the door on his side and saw Deb's door was ajar so he pushed it open. Deb was sleeping. He tiptoed to the bed and bent over to kiss her forehead.

"Glen!" Deb said reaching up to pull him near.

"Whoops!" He lost his balance and landed half on her.

"I missed you so." Deb said.

He wrapped his arms around her. "It's a good thing you did miss me, I would have crushed you if I had fallen on you, silly."

"Take a nap with me." She slid over to make room.

"Is it ok? Are you strong? I've been thinking of you all the way so be warned." Glen slipped of his shoes and shirt off stretching out on top of the covers. "Mmmm, I can feel I'm in your warm spot." He slipped under the covers snuggling close

"Not yet," she teased "but this will have to do."

They napped for an hour. He thought it was a dream when he woke and Deb was there beside him. He moved a bit to be sure he wasn't dreaming. It was really she, in the flesh. "Control, control yourself, man." He told himself. "Deb?" He whispered.

"Mmmm?" She answered. "Mmmm, this feels wonderful." They stretched next to each other. "You need to get up or we'll have a problem." He pulled her closer. Their heartbeats mingled. "Please get up, Deb." He pushed her away.

"Me? This is my bed! You get up." She threw the spread off, going into the bathroom. She put on a pants-and-sweater outfit. Glen just watched and smiled. He'd put on his shoes and shirt. "Did you know that you just dressed in front of me? What a hussy!"

"You liked it, though." It seemed natural. There was no shyness or shame dressing in front of him.

"Yes." He walked toward the adjoining door.

"Wait!" Deb grabbed him and kissed his face and lips. "There, now you can go. Want to go for a drink before the boys come?"

"Want to," he grinned.

❦ CHAPTER 25 ❦

THEY SAT ON THE SAME SIDE of a booth near the door so they could see Deb's sons when they came. "There they are." Deb waved. Deb and Glen slid out of the booth and she hugged each of her sons. Then turned to introduce them to Glen. Tall as her sons were, they looked up to him. They all sat down again making small talk for a while and then Dan, Jr. turned to Glen. "Tell me, Mr. Jarvis, what are your intentions concerning our mother?"

Without flinching, Glen turned to him. "You may call me Glen if you wish. My intentions are entirely indecent except that I plan to marry your mother and make them decent and legal." He took her hand and smiled. "I want to spend the rest of our lives caring for her, being with her if she'll let me."

Dan and Jay both laughed. "Dan, I like this guy, "Jay said. "I see why Mom does."

"Do you fellows know a decent place to get a good steak?" Glen was on his way to winning over her sons. Deb loved it.

Their choices ended with a favorite western bar down the street where it was noisy and fun but the steaks were good. They had a beer, steaks and laughed a lot. Glen and the boys got into a friendly banter over their favorite athletic teams. Glen soon turned to Deb. "We're leaving you out, dear."

"I'm learning a lot. Besides, I enjoy listening to my three favorite males getting to know each other." They appreciated that and went on with their discussion. It took a couple of hours to eat and visit.

After dinner, they were back at the parking lot where the vehicles were. Dan and Jay each shook Glen's hand vigorously and said they were glad to meet him. They each hugged their mom and said they approved of her man and were happy for them. Deb and Glen said they planned to stay for the weekend so they invited Deb's Sons to join them whenever they could. She was pleased when Dan invited them to join him at his church Sunday morning and they agreed to meet him there.

Jay said he'd call the next day and meet them with his son, six-year-old Jake. The boys left and Glen and Deb went inside to her room to visit awhile. Glen took his shoes and socks off. It looked like that was becoming one of their rituals. He stretched out his legs, using the bed for a footrest. Deb propped up on the pillows, covering their feet with the spread.

It was the first time they'd been able to just talk and share something besides business. This reminded them of the time in the motel before Mark's wedding. "In fact, it was in Fargo!" It was a memory that would always remain precious to them. When it was bedtime, Glen reminded Deb that he wouldn't always leave her room at bedtime. She said she looked forward to just that in six weeks or so. There was more "business" talk but would wait until tomorrow. Sharing a meaningful hug, he went to his room.

Deb woke and went into Glen's room with an orange to

share. Sitting on his bed, she woke him with the pungent odor emitted by peeling an orange. He rolled over. "What are you doing wicked woman, trying to entice me with your fruit?" She pulled off a section and offered it to him. He opened his mouth and they laughed as she popped it in then kissed him.

They decided to have a swim before breakfast. They'd meet at pool side. Deb noticed again that Glen had kept himself in good physical shape. She told him so as they slipped into the water. He said there was a time he was pretty sad-looking and feeling out of shape. So he went on a fitness program and plans to stay on it.

Glen told Deb he appreciated she cared about her physical self and thought she looked ten years younger than her age, well maybe eight years being an older woman. Deb told him she belonged to a fitness club for over twenty years. They both said they wanted to continue a form of fitness together after they were married.

They agreed that physical appeal was not what made a person. Yet it was good to care about ones health. Swimsuits hid no flaws. She knew she had gotten thicker in the body but had always made an effort to keep her weight down in spite of her love for sweets, chocolate in particular, she mostly ate healthy food.

They swam several laps. Deb showed Glen her favorite form of complete relaxation. "You get into the deep water and lay your head back letting your body float in the water. Only the face is out of the water. The free–flowing weightlessness soothes a person. Sounds are muffled as the water covers your ears." He tried it and liked it too. Challenging each other to see who could tread water the longest, they decided to call it a draw at ten minutes and promised to try again in the pool at his townhouse.

After breakfast, it was time to talk wedding plans again. Deb told Glen the problem with the seniors feeling badly because they would miss the wedding ceremony. Being the sweet thoughtful person he was, he agreed to have the ceremony in the sanctuary instead of the chapel and "Have them all there, the whole town if you wish as long as we're married when it's over." They both laughed and Deb hugged him and told him how wonderful he was.

Planning to get rid of more inventory, they continued to write it all down so it wouldn't have to be discussed again.

A change of scene was needed so they walked over to the mall. Mostly they walked and talked window shopping. A couple whom Deb knew from her lay ministry training program were there. She introduced them to Glen, for the first time, as "my fiancee." They visited for a while and as they walked away, Glen took her hand and tucked it under his arm, close to him. "Thank you for that. It sounded strange but I felt so proud, honey."

"We could go back to the motel and you could show me how thankful you are or take me to a movie or something?" Deb teased.

"We need to be out in public with lots of people around." Glen insisted. So they chose a matinee sharing popcorn and a drink for their lunch. They held hands when they ran out of popcorn.

Jay had called and invited them to join him for supper. He would have his son, Jake with him. He was divorced now but worked hard at being a dad to Jake. So they all met at a pizza place. After the pizza was devoured, Glen went off to "rescue" Jake from the game room. They took quite a while using up all of Glen's quarters.

While they were gone, Jay said. "Mom, I really like Glen. You seem so right for each other. He is very different from Dad. He is kind and tender and I can see how he feels about you just by the way he looks at you." He grabbed his mother's hand. "Mom, I just want you to be happy. I know it's been a long time since you loved or were loved. You have a right to claim some happiness."

"Thank you, Jay. It means a lot to both of us to have your approval. I want you and Jake will be able to come to our wedding. But I do know it is the holidays, the busiest time for you." Jay was in the entertainment business, booking bands and DJs for every kind of business and private event. He had used a contact in Grand Island to book a DJ he knew for Deb and Glen's reception. Deb told him she was grateful .She knew they were usually booked months ahead especially during the holidays. He considered it his wedding present to furnish the DJ and wouldn't let them pay for it.

"I would love to be there for you Mom, but it probably won't happen. So know that I wish you the most happiness possible. Just be sure, Mom."

Glen and Jake were coming with ice cream cones so the conversation ended. "Jake insisted we all liked chocolate best so you have one choice."

"Right on!" Jay and Grandma echoed as they dug in.

Sunday morning, Glen shared another orange Deb had brought along, then left to meet Dan at his church. His pick up was in the parking lot so the couple went inside. Dan was visiting with the pastor and started toward them as he saw his Mom and her. The pastor came with him. "Pastor, you've met my Mom, Deb Sullivan and this is her intended, Glen Jarvis."

"And what do you intend?" Pastor Mitchell laughed and shook Glen's hand.

Glen was laughing too. "I intend to marry Deb."

"Well, congratulations to both of you." He shook Deb's hand now.

After worship Dan invited them to brunch at a restaurant close by. Glen asked that thanks be given. He gave thanks for family and relationships that were developing and that the Lord would bless each of them through Jesus Christ. Dan raised an eyebrow and threw his mother a glance. Deb smiled at him as she raised her head and said "Amen. Thank you, Glen." Dan said "Amen" with her.

While they ate, Deb and Glen explained the unplanned "pomp' that was fast growing for their wedding. Dan laughed and told Glen that he had better get used to things like this. He said he believed his mother had some magnet that caused simple things to become complicated. Glen nodded in agreement.

Deb pretended to be insulted and the guys laughed at her. Then Deb and Glen asked Dan to walk his mother down the aisle. He said he'd be honored. They also asked him to help host the reception with Carol and Peg and their husbands. He liked that too.

In the parking lot, they each hugged the other good bye and got into separate vehicles to go different directions. Dan, Jr. was leaving town too. He was a representative for a large food preparation company so he was on his way to South Dakota.

⚔ CHAPTER 26 ⚔

AS SHE SET THE CRUISE ON the van, Deb had a deja vou feeling. How many more times would they drive away from each other? The trip home gave Deb time to reminisce about the last two months particularly this last weekend.

I am so grateful that my sons like Glen since for them, this is the man who will take the place of their father in my life. They knew what Dan's and my marriage had been for many years. Dan, Jr might have had a problem, since he is most like his father, intense and serious, on guard with strangers. He was more accepting of his father's rigid control. He still insisted that kind of philosophy made a responsible and disciplined person. We'd had some tense discussions when I told him I planned to divorce his father. He not only argued with me but with himself. He thought I should stick it out even if there was no love or happiness possible. Then, when Dan died, he expected me to feel guilty, as if "my wish came true." It took him a long time to agree it wasn't my fault that his father died.

At the same time, Dan has my sense of humor, which goes a long way to help him lighten up. Maybe it will help him relate to Glen. .

Jay thought his dad's death gave his mother a chance to be free and find peace. He is more carefree and open, could sit for hours with a perfect stranger and talk as if he had known him forever. Jay never understood his father's need for control, so he had a hard time having a relationship with him. He would appreciate a man like Glen in my life. Though they only had several hours to get to know each other, Glen had a way with people that gained their trust and respect. Yet. If my sons had reservations about Glen, they loved me enough to want my happiness, and were willing to give him a chance.

Three down, one to go. We'd accomplish that when we went to Carol's for Thanksgiving. I have no doubt that Carol would like Glen. She, more than any of my kids, is most like me. She wears her feelings on her sleeves, and is loving and emotional, laughs and cries easily. Like her mother, she gets a lot of exercise "jumping to conclusions", and then feeling sorry later.

She never had much of a relationship with her father so she seldom got caught up in his control world. She was strong-willed and determined to survive it all. Though she never gave up wanting his love, I doubt she ever felt it.

A degree of tough love would best describe Carol's approach to parenting. Though it hurt her, she often let her daughters live the consequences of their behavior good or bad. She is fiercely protective of her family but wants to mold them into responsible adults some day.

Carol married her college sweetheart. Kevin, her husband is her grandfather image, rather than her father. He tries to be a tough German like my dad was, yet is really a tender and loving husband and father. Bathrooms full of women's stuff and a houseful of female moods and personalities, still keep him from having a problem being the only male in the family. He taught his three daughters to play ball and climb trees and fix cars. In a sweet way, he like most men, is totally confused by the whole female thing.

Carol and Kevin both teach and coach in the Parochial School their daughters attend. So their whole family is busy coming and going different directions. They work hard at their marriage and family, making ends meet and keeping up with the whirlwind created by three talented girls.

Time flew like the miles with her mind preoccupied so. The sun beat in the window adding to the warm glow of for family and now her Fiancée. She's in love and engaged at her age. Who would have dreamed it?

Glen accelerated as he blended into the traffic on the interstate, set the cruise and heaved a sigh of relief. Lots of traffic Sunday afternoons, he thought. One kid left to go. Actually, he thought *it went quite well. I would have guessed the sons would be the most challenging. They would naturally want to protect their mom and preserve their family name. Deb was smart to not give me a clue to the boys' personalities or make up. I appreciate that she wanted me to find out for myself.*

The older son, Dan, Jr., acts more serious, a lot like Dan, Sr. Yet, Glen felt they hit it off well. The positive is he loves his mom and cares about her welfare. He also has his mother's sense of humor. Glen appreciated his openness. I am sure I will always know where I stood with Dan.

Jay seems more easy-going and friendly. Glen guessed he needs more love and gives it more easily. He certainly showed it to his mom and his son. He seems like a one on one person. Jay will be interesting to get to know. He is likeable.

Deb assured me that child number four would be the easiest to get to know. Easy for Deb to say! Carol comes with a husband and three daughters, all of whom have opinions. Deb could never brag enough about Carol's girls. I have to admit, I look forward to meeting them after hearing so much about them. This whole family is starting to get to me. It feels good to be a part of them. This is quite a package I am marrying into.

We'll get the trip to Omaha over and then our engagement party my friends have planned. That is probably as nerve wracking for her as meeting her family is for me. I could tell her not to worry, they already love her. Before she leaves, we'll complete the family rounds for now with breakfast with Tami, my step daughter and family. Wow! I was pleased that Tami was so accepting of Deb.

I have my job to wind down now. My partners, Jim and Greg know about it but I need have closure with the rest of the office personnel and be done by the end of the year. I'm really looking forward to retirement. Deb and I discussed it and she agreed that I keep my fingers in a bit by computer in my storage room, soon to be home office. Jim, my partner was hoping so since that was really his idea. He wants to pick my brain from time to time. I never thought I'd retire. But then, I never thought I'd fall in love in my sixties and want my time for myself and my woman.

I still have to finish our honeymoon plans. All I've told Deb is to pack for a month and bring all kinds of weather clothes. She hasn't been as curious as I thought she would.

Home again, Deb had two major tasks. One was leaving her job. It means saying goodbye to those dear shut-ins at least as their chaplain. There was good news to bring them though about our marriage ceremony. Each of them would be personally invited. Every effort would be made to see to it they were there as guests. Two limousines and one handicapped van would drive them to the wedding at the church and then to the reception at the hotel.

Her other job was finishing the wedding and reception details. Forty years ago, my wedding was different. She thought she knew all the answers then. Huh, she didn't even know the questions.

Dan's parents were adamant about him marrying when he had so much school left. His father especially was against it, not Deb but just the timing. Her parents expressed reservations out loud too. They were disappointed that Deb would postpone her education and support them until Dan finished medical school, then residency all of which would take their little family more than a thousand miles from home. She could only understand how they felt when her own kids married and left home for good.

Now her children and grandchildren were going to witness this wedding. Unbelievable! Deb was old enough now to appreciate that a wedding is an event that would mean a change in her life. *We marry for different reasons at different times in our lives. I married Dan out of passion and to get away from home for a different life. I will marry Glen for love and companionship. Neither of us have expectations about the other. We just want to have someone, not be alone. Love makes it special.*

Her friend, Sherry Jansen is a wedding coordinator, so she called her for some help. Glen left those details up to Deb but she did honor requests he had. One of which was no soloist singing some love song at the wedding. So she planned to have the guests join them to sing some appropriate hymns.

They both preferred a small intimate wedding but there were too many people who wanted to be there and Glen had generously agreed to a church full.

Glen's job was the honeymoon. In spite of Deb's prodding he insisted on a secret though he had a hard time concealing his excitement. Glen and Deb phoned every day just to keep in touch but they did have business to discuss.

⚔ CHAPTER 27 ⚔

IT SEEMED A MATTER OF DAYS until Deb was getting off the plane in St. Paul again, searching for Glen's face again. Her heart still jumped when she saw him leaning against the wall, easy to spot with his head above the crowd. His eyes met hers. He grinned and they reached for each other. This time Deb had bags to pick up. In airports someone is always arriving or leaving so you see lots of hugs and kisses in public. Deb and Glen did too.

Stopping at a restaurant for breakfast, they soon were back on the highway. Omaha was five hours away so they'd be there by early afternoon. They talked wedding and moving and merging of property business just to get that out of the way. Deb laid her head under Glen's arm and napped for half an hour. He gently touched her cheek. "Deb, we're close to Omaha. Will you wake up and guide me to your kid's house?"

"Mm huh." She moaned and hugged him, sat up and kissed his cheek. "Yes, my love, I will."

They pulled into the Welchs yard and three young ladies appeared before they could get out of the car. They had to be watching for them. The girls staged a crazy dance routine on the huge porch as Glen parked. Deb jumped out her side and did her usual group hug with the girls, first while Glen watched and laughed and then he was brought into the circle. Glen fell in love with that trio at that moment.

Stepping back, Deb introduced Glen. First there was Julie, thirteen tall and lanky, poised and almost shy with her country-girl beauty and strawberry-blonde hair and freckles. She's an athlete and musical. Being the oldest has given her the "setting an example" position which she resents at times but lives up to.

Emily at ten was already the jock in the family. Every season, she has a sport to give her passion to. She plays softball, basketball, volleyball and soccer. Her hair is short and neat and she dresses plain and comfortably. At this age, she is already the best pianist in the family. She is sensitive like her mom so it is hard for her to be competitive but she gears up for it.

Then there is willowy, impish Mara who is nine. She runs or tries to run the family as well as the world. Her determination and strength can be offensive at times, especially to her older sisters and often becomes a challenge to her parents. Yet, she has genuine leadership ability. Loving and friendly, everyone likes her.

Glen bowed slightly and shook each girl's hand, repeating her name. They beamed and giggled.

Carol and Kevin watched from the doorway waiting for the girls to "have their turn. Then they came bounding out the door. Well, Carol did. Kevin, more conservative, came behind her. Everyone helped unload the car. There was soup and fresh bread for lunch. The adults sat visiting at the big round table in the large country kitchen. It was reminiscent of Glen's parents kitchen.

Deb told Glen how Carol and Kevin had completely restored and remodeled this big old country home. Being a building contractor, Glen showed such interest that Kevin took him on a house tour. Carol and her mother cleared the lunch dishes and she told Deb how impressed she was with Glen. She hugged her mother.

Thanksgiving Community Worship Wednesday evening was followed by pizza in town. Back home, they played a game of golf, the card version.

Deb felt herself fading and Glen looked tired so Deb inquired as to sleeping arrangements. Mara wanted to know if Glen was going to sleep with her Grandma. Before her parents could register their disapproval of her question, Glen explained.

"No, we can't because we aren't married."

"Are you going to get married?" She asked.

Embarrassed, her father said. "Mara!"

"Well, I need to know." She insisted.

Glen winked at Deb and reached for her hand. He showed Mara her Grandma's ring. "We are engaged and we want to get married. Would that be ok with you?"

"Grandma!" They exclaimed almost together. Before Mara could reply, Emily turned to Glen. "Will you be our Grandpa then?" Glen squeezed Deb's hand and looked straight at Emily. "I'd like that, would you?"

"Yeah!" Both Emily and Mara echoed. Julie just shook her head.

Carol said the other two girls would bunk together and "Glen could have Emily's room while he is here. Though the bed probably won't be long enough."

"'I'm used to that." Glen shared. "I just..." He stretched his long legs across the room and wiggled his feet, let my toes hang over the end of the bed." They all laughed with him.

Thanksgiving Day dawned, white and wintry. It had snowed during the night. Carol and Deb got the pies done and popped the turkey in the oven before they could play. So the girls set the table to hurry them. Everyone dressed in warm clothes and went out to make angels in the snow. Deb and her granddaughters hadn't done that together for years.

Glen told the girls he hadn't made a snow angel since he was Julie's age. They couldn't believe it. They told him that when they and their grandma get snow at the same time, they all agree to go outside and make angels in the snow even though they're hundreds of miles apart. They would have to teach Glen how. The girls proceeded to demonstrate with him as their model. He was as impossible as could be and they all laughed until they fell in a heap in the snow. There was voting on who had the best angel. Glen won for size only and Emily's was the most perfectly shaped angel.

Their huge yard was perfect for the Fox and Hound Game. Loud discussion about the rules finally got Grandma Deb involved. She declared herself the referee settling the disputes before all of the snow was gone.

The moms went in to work on dinner after that. The

rest of the "kids" weren't through yet. Kevin and Glen got into a snowball fight with the girls. There was lots of yelling, screaming and laughing going on out there. They all came into the porch to strip off the sopping clothes and continue arguing over who won.

After dinner, the guys played board games with the girls and half-watched football and everyone dozed occasionally.

Friday, they all packed into the Welchs van and joined the holiday throng at the mall. Their family did little shopping but enjoyed the bustle of the other dedicated shoppers. The day ended with a Holiday Matinee at the I-MAX Theater.

Saturday, Kevin wanted to show Deb and Glen the sights around Omaha. One was the Strategic Air Command Museum. Glen had not seen it and was especially interested since he had been in the air force. He and Kevin went off on their own to view history from the nuclear missile days. The women and girls soon ended up in the gift shop and waited in the coffee shop.

It was time to tell the Welchs of Deb and Glen's wedding plans. They already knew Carol and Kevin and the girls were coming to Grand Island for Christmas but hadn't told them a wedding was planned while they were there.

Grandma Deb was requested to share bedtime moments with her grand daughters and would gather the rest of her things together. No matter how old they were, the girls loved the bedtime ritual of talk, prayer, maybe singing a hymn. It was Glen's chance to talk to Carol alone while Kevin tended chores outside.

He began. "Carol, you probably can tell I love your mom very much. I would like you to help me with something though."

"I'll be happy to, Glen but what could that be?"

"Well," he hesitated, "I know that your mom had a lot of pain in her marriage to your father. I even met him so I can only imagine. I don't know how much you were aware of but I assume she shared a lot of it with you since you are so close."

"Yes, she did. My dad was not an easy person to live with, not for Mom or for us. She has been so much happier since she has been single.

Glen tried to explain. "That is my concern."

"But Glen, you know her now as a happier person than you would have known years ago. How can that be a problem?"

"I know happiness and contentment has been hers in single life. I want her to stay happy. I want to give her all the love and companionship that we both desire and yet still allow her to have her privacy and aloneness that she reveres. I have been alone for eight years, so I have had enough solitude. It scares me a bit that I might interfere in her need for privacy. I want our marriage to give her all of that amd yet have togetherness."

Tears filled Carol's eye. "Glen, you just answered your own question. Don't you see? You recognize Mom's need for privacy and you love her enough to want to assure that for her."

"I hope so, Carol. I wouldn't want to assume she would give that up for me."

Carol sobbed a combination of a cry and a laugh. "She loves you enough to want to give up most of it. Her needs for privacy and aloneness were some of her way of avoiding the hurt of her relationship with my dad. You see, she doesn't need that any more." Carol reached her arms out and Glen enfolded her.

"Thank you, Carol. I think I understand that. It helps."

Looking into his face, Carol said. "Thank God, Mom has a man like you in her life, that she won't just have someone but she has someone to love. Thank you."

Deb came into the room as they stepped apart, she heard their last remarks. "So, what have we, a conspiracy of some kind?'

"Yes, Mom." Carol reached out to enfold her mom in their circle. "Yes, we are conspiring to ensure your happiness with Glen."

"You said it!" Glen agreed.

"You are, both of you." Deb stood back and looked at two of her most favorite people in the world. "I love you both." She declared and all of them cried.

Kevin came in and said, "Can I join this happy occasion?" They all laughed and hugged each other. That broke the tension. "Thank you, Kevin for lightening us up." His mother-in-law hugged him. "You know what sentimental fools Carol and I are."

"Yes." He turned to Glen. "I've seen them in action before. It's usually worse."

The four of them sat to discuss details of the wedding. Deb told Carol that she wanted her and Peg to stand up for them. Glen said he had asked his nephews to stand up for him. Kevin and Carol offered to help in any way. Glen also asked the young couple if they would share host duties at the reception with Peg and Ron and Dan, Jr. They were assured there would be work to do when they got to Grand Island for Christmas. Glen told them he was really looking forward to a Sullivan Family Christmas.

Deb reminded Kevin to bring a trailer or the truck for "Mom's Giveaways."

He only groaned.

Sunday morning, the family took an entire pew in the little country church the Welchs belonged to. In the parking lot, hugs and kisses, and promises to be together for Christmas and the wedding in Grand Island ended the weekend. As they pulled away from each other, they waved from the church yard. Once onto the interstate, Glen reached his arm around Deb. She snuggled close."Everything you said about your daughter's family is true but you could have bragged more. They are wonderful."

"So are you, Glen. I knew you'd say that. They fell in love with you. You just amaze me the way you do the right thing to endear people to you."

"Like what? I only acted like me."

"Oh, I know. That's what is so special about you. You just act naturally for you and they all melt, like not knowing how to make angels in the snow." She pointed out.

"I was telling the truth. It must be forty or fifty years since I did that."

"You were extremely difficult to teach the game to and impossible at making a snow angel."

He chuckled, "Yeah, but it's not easy to learn when you're

old. You know about teaching old dogs. Apparently, I don't have the talent for making snow angels."

"Right!" Deb agreed. She loved him more every day.

❈ CHAPTER 28 ❈

THEY GOT BACK TO GLEN'S WITH just enough time to change for their engagement party at Judy and Floyd Martin's home. They lived in one of the townhouses several doors away from Glen's so they walked. The fresh crisp air felt good. Glen was right about the party. There were twenty-five or thirty people there, many of whom Deb had met at the brunch a month ago. The others were people Glen worked with and church members.

A mock wedding was staged, with faded plastic flowers and weeds. The bride wore a dirty white tulle nightgown with a lace peignoir over it. A worn curtain was held in place by a foil-covered pie tin. The groom was attired in a green plaid leisure suit. A soloist sang an out-of-tune version of "Bridge Over Troubled Waters" The hood of a dark brown shroud, more appropriate for a funeral, covered the preacher's face completely. The actors portrayed the real bride and groom's mannerisms well. When the preacher came to the part where he asked for the rings, everyone pulled out a bell and rang it.

Though Deb and Glen had requested no gifts there was a pile of them to open. They were gag gifts. One was of value though, a telephone book with "important" numbers highlighted, like doctors, hospitals, emergency rooms, nursing homes, mortuaries, cemeteries, but also travel agencies. There were tabs marking retirement homes, marriage counselors, divorce lawyers, and bankruptcy accountants. Each one of the guests had written their own names and addresses on the inside cover so Deb and Gen wouldn't forget them. That was one of the more useful gifts.

In addition to many "necessary" bathroom items; they received "wearing apparel" that was supposed to be "appropriate" for the wedding night.

There was also a traveler's survival kit for the honeymoon. It contained the usual emergency items like Band-Aids and aspirins. But also laxatives, Lomotil, antacids, vitamins, sun screen, a huge jar of Vaseline, earplugs, etc. They included books like "Sex for Dummies" and The Joys of Sex Over Sixty" and "How to Deal With Difficult People" which might become "necessary reading.".

The final gift was a six-pack of pills for "male sexual dysfunction." Glen joked that he wouldn't need it once Deb gave in to his charms. He blushed then. Some of his friends were surprised to even hear him talk that way. Deb told them she was going to keep the pills "just in case" and that she planned to stay on the pill so she wouldn't get pregnant, then she blushed.

A game involved everyone giving them advice on marriage. Glen and Deb gave them each an invitation to their wedding with a list of accommodations in Grand Island and directions to Deb's house and the church. A wonderful dinner was served.

With bags of gifts in hand, the honored couple left for Glen's. Once there, they were too wired to sleep, so they sat in front of the fireplace with shoes off and feet up and reminisced about the events of the last few days. Glen was proud that his friends loved Deb. They made her look forward to their part in her life. Deb assured Glen that her family accepted him. How blessed they were with family and friends.

"Oh." Glen jumped up. "Before we argue over who sleeps in my bed, I have something for you." He handed her a large pink box with a huge bow. Inside was a plush pink terry velour bathrobe with matching slippers. Under it was a soft satin night-gown of pink and white stripes.

"Oh, this is wonderful! It's beautiful!" Deb scooped them all up.

"Try them. See if they fit,"

She stepped into Glen's room and came back, sashaying as a model would. She laughed and landed close to Glen on the sofa. "Thank you. You are so good to me. I love it." She hugged him.

"Actually," he sounded serious, "I had a problem with you wearing out my shirt and socks. Mmmm, you feel so soft." He hugged her.

Deb slept on the sofa again, one last time. They both got up early even though Deb's flight back to Grand Island wasn't until late afternoon. They had their date with Tami and her family so they left taking only what Deb had to take to Grand Island. She might as well leave what she could at Glen's.

They had a very pleasant meal with Tami, her husband Jonathan, who took off time from his job to join them, and their two children. A boy named Allen had to be six years old. He had lost several front teeth. Deb joked with him about it as soon as she found out he wasn't sensitive about it. His three year old sister, Mackenzie had chosen her own clothes for the event. She had on a bright red skirt, an orange top and blue socks with sandals. Her mother said that "Kinzy" is very clothes conscious. It was a happy occasion, especially with the children and they called Glen Grandpa so they asked if they could call Deb, Grandma. "I would be honored" she declared. "I have six other grand children and would love to have two more." The children beamed.

Deb kissed Glen good-bye one more time at the airport. This was less enjoyable every time. Not for long though. This was the last time she would leave him this way.

❧ CHAPTER 29 ❧

GLEN PLANNED TO FINISH HIS LAST week of work at his office by December 20th, and then he would drive over to Grand Island to help Deb pack and sort. He would stay until after the wedding. Deb had already done some packing and sorting but there was still a lot to get through and Christmas company would help decide what would happen to other things. The kids could claim what they wanted before it went to auction. He also knew Deb was excited to have her family in her home one last time before it got sold too.

One thing that hadn't decided was how to handle physical desires and a sleeping arrangement while he would be in Grand Island before the wedding. Peg had offered to have him stay at her place. That seemed like a good solution.

He had to pack for the honeymoon too before he left, so he was ready for that when they came back after the wedding. He had to remember Christmas and wedding gifts. He planned to wear his navy suit that Deb liked for the wedding. He chuckled as he packed casual clothes. Deb had work for him, packing for her move to St. Paul.

He wondered *what kind of holiday traditions Deb's family had. He hadn't really spent Christmas in a family setting for several years. Connie, his sister-in-law, had invited him to be with her and his nephews and family several times, but now she was married so he felt like an intruder. Pastor Dave and other friends in St. Paul had included him in family gatherings like a holiday meal. His step children always spent the holidays with their dad now that their mother had died. The gift exchange party celebration would be different. Deb's whole family would be there so it will be a crowd. He had a feeling it would be a noisy, rollicking crowd just getting them all under one roof. If he knew Deb, she had every meal planned and nearly ready by now. She liked to enjoy the company too rather than spend her time in the kitchen.*

Finally on his way, Glen took the Interstate 90 wondering what he forgot. So many things would be happening in the next month, he was sure he had forgotten something. But at least he was sure he had remembered the wedding details.

It seemed only a few days since he first drove to Grand Island in September. In those three months, not long, he could not remember life before Deb. It seemed only a few days since he first called her.

Now he would have holidays and family and trips and companionship as never before. All life will be different with Deb in his life.

The car was loaded down and he was on his way by seven o'clock. He should be in Grand Island by suppertime at least.

He was about twenty miles from Bismarck when he looked

up to see a truck coming off a ramp. Glen was sure the driver didn't see him, the way he was coming. He was going too fast. Glen moved to the passing lane but the driver continued into his path. Finally, he was in the median when they collided. Thoughts went through his head at breakneck speed. *Gotta get out of the way, speed up, slow down, he's going to hit me.*

There was the sound of glass and metal in slow motion. A bump that didn't seem so hard and the next thing he remembered, he was being slid out of the driver's side of the car. There were voices that seemed muffled and slow. He could feel himself moving but he wasn't helping, like floating. Faces swam before his eyes, then more faces. Voices were loud and demanding like broken, injury, bleeding, X-ray, vital, blood pressure. Someone was calling his name or did he just think it. "Glen! Glen, can you hear me?" He could hear but couldn't respond though he tried. He tried to connect, none of it made sense. Something hurt, but what? He tried to connect, answer, make sense of it. He fought it but sleep overcame him. Now darkness and silence.

The name Deb kept coming up, Deb, Deb, was he just thinking it. Deb, was he saying it or was someone else? Deb, where are you? He quit fighting it and slept.

Then he was jostled around again, lights, hallways, voices. He couldn't fight, he slept again.

✕ CHAPTER 30 ✕

DEB BUSIED HERSELF STRAIGHTENING THE HOUSE and watching the time. Glen was leaving early this morning, so he should be in Grand Island by suppertime. She had a small roast ready to bake for dinner.

About 3 o'clock, the phone rang. A male voice asked if this was Deb Sullivan. When she said yes, he identified himself as a highway patrolman in Bismarck. Her knees went weak.

"Oh, no" was all she could say. She sank into a chair. Thoughts of his next statement raced through her head.

He said, "Mr. Glen Jarvis has been taken to the hospital here in Bismarck. I don't know the extent of his injuries, but he is alive. I'm sorry to have to call and tell you this. He has been saying your name over and over. I found your phone number in his wallet."

He told her Glen's car had been sideswiped by a truck. He could tell her more following the investigation.

"I'll be there as soon as I can. Where is he? Which hospital?" The patrolman told her he was at St. As. She thanked him. He said he was sorry again. They hung up.

Deb grabbed a bag, threw some essentials in it, turned back for the cell phone, and left. All the way there, she kept thinking *I had doubts about our rushing into this relationship, especially marriage. Like do we need more time to be sure, get to know each other better? I argued with myself about that for weeks, even though I knew I loved him. This love was so different from what I felt for Dan. It was a new experience, more exciting. Yet at the same time, calm, quiet and deep. Some of that was probably due to our "mature" stage of life, There seemed a mutual caring, a give-and-take that we shared. I couldn't remember ever feeling that way about Dan. Life felt complete with Glen and yet there was that uncertainty inside for both of us, that we should slow down, take our time. What could you expect from a person who took forty years getting out of a dysfunctional marriage? I couldn't be accused of being impulsive. Glen and I had talked about it more than once. If either of us had any doubts, we'd call it off or at least postpone our marriage. There may never be complete certainty of anything as far as human nature goes. This accident did it for me. The thought of losing him was unbearable.*

What a cruel trick to be this near to a perfect love and then lose it. I don't care how long it takes for him to recover. I don't care how long I will have him. I want every moment to count.

"Dear God," she prayed, "I know you are in charge, and I am glad for that. You know what I need and should have, what about our future. If it is your will, keep him for me so we may know some time for our love. I will take him any way he is, for as long as you provide. Give him to me as you see fit, whatever you think I can handle. Just give me my love to love for a time." She prayed and sang familiar hymns that gave her comfort.

Now she recalled what life was like before he came back into her life. She cried and prayed, thanked and pleaded. She was halfway there when she thought of calling Peg and Carol, Jay and Dan, and Glen's stepchildren too. She called Carol, she'd be home and she can call the others later. At the sound of her voice, Deb began crying.

"Mom, what is it? Are you ok?"

"It's not me, Carol, It's Glen," and then she really sobbed. "Glen has been in an accident near Bismarck. I'm on my way now. I don't know any more about it yet. Carol, call the kids and start praying."

"Immediately, Mom. Yes, we will, Mom. Call me later when you can. I'll call our family. Who else should I call? What about Glen's people?"

"I can call Peg right now, dear but I will let you call the boys. I don't know, Carol, I can't think. Maybe you could call Central Lutheran in St. Paul and talk to Pastor Dave Hanson. He will know who else."

"Yes, Mom. I'll do what I can. Talk to you later. You drive safely now. I love you." They hung up. Deb felt numb like she was in a fog. She cried some more.

❧ CHAPTER 31 ❧

DEB PARKED NEAR THE EMERGENCY AREA and hurried to the desk to ask about Glen. The nurse said he was in X-ray or surgery. But he would probably be in Intensive Care before she could see him.

"What happened, how bad is it? Do you know?" She had lots of questions. The nurse was kind but firm. "You will have to talk to the doctor. He will come here to talk to you." She showed her to a lounge and offered a cup of coffee.

"No, thank you." She just sat feeling numb. The nurse brought a glass of water. Deb asked if there was a chaplain on call. The nurse said she would contact one.

In five minutes, Chaplain Curtis came into the room. He introduced himself and Deb told him her name was Deb Sullivan and her fiancée had just been in an auto/truck collision. He said he was sorry and then said, "Did you say your fiancée?"

She realized how silly that must seem, a woman of her age.

"Yes, we are to be married after Christmas." He looked expectant, so she went on. "We seem a bit old, I suppose, but we met each other thirty-some years ago, and since then have both been married to others and just met again several months ago. It is a dream come true."

"How wonderful for you both!"

"Chaplain, would you pray with me about Glen and me?"

"Certainly."

"There is a special verse that means a lot to me. It's in 2nd Corinthians, chapter four. I can't remember exactly, but it tells about not being defeated, not losing heart. I think it starts at verse five or six. Would you read that to me?

"Yes, I know it." He leafed through his Bible. "Yes, here it is, beginning at verse six:

'For it is God who has commanded light to shine-out of darkness,

Who has shown in our hearts to give light in the knowledge

Of the glory of God in the face of Jesus Christ.

For we have this treasure in earthen vessels,

That the excellence of power may be of God and not of us.

We are hard-pressed on every side, yet not crushed,

We are perplexed, but not in despair.

Persecuted but not forsaken, struck down but not destroyed.

Always carrying about in the body the dying of the Lord Jesus Christ,

That the life of Jesus may be manifested in our body.

For we who live are always delivered to death for Jesus's sake,

That the life of Jesus also may be manifested in our mortal flesh.

So death is at work in us but life also is at work in us.

Since we have the same spirit of faith according to what has been written,

"I believe therefore I spoke." We also speak because we believe.

Knowing that He who raised up the Lord Jesus will also raise us up with Jesus, And will present us.

For all things are for your sake, that grace, having spread through many,

May cause thanksgiving to abound to the glory of God.

Therefore we do not lose heart, even though our outward person is perishing, Yet inwardly we are being renewed day by day.

For our affliction which is but for a moment,

is working for us an exceeding weight of glory. .

We do not look at the things that are seen,

But at the things which are not seen. For the things which are seen are temporary but the things which are not seen are eternal.'"

"Yes," She said and was silent. After a few minutes, Chaplain Curtis handed her his Testament marked on that spot.

"What a fitting Bible reading. How did you know? It is God's word and promise, pleading and thanking all at once?"

"I am a lay chaplain in Grand Island. I use that verse or parts of it for those whom I care. It is fitting for all of us but especially those hurting ones."

He put his hand on her arm and prayed for Glen and

Deb, that their love would endure this event, and love of the Lord would give them strength and comfort to see it through. Both Deb and the chaplain said "Amen." Then he said he would wait with her if she wanted him to. Deb said that wasn't necessary, but she would appreciate him or another chaplain calling on Glen later.

"Of course, be happy to. Blessings to you and I pray Glen recovers well." He left. It seemed hours until the doctor came into the waiting room. "Deb, Deb Sullivan?" He asked.

"Yes?"

"So it's you Glen has been speaking of. He called your name often. The patrolman found your last name in his wallet so we could call you."

"Oh." She felt weak again. "So what happened? How is Glen? Will he be all right?"

The doctor first said "he's banged up some but is in good health otherwise so his prognosis is good. We will keep him in ICU overnight just to monitor him.

"What a relief!" Deb still felt weak.

"According to the attending patrolman, a truck went out of control. His brakes failed. He plowed into Glen's car as he came down a ramp outside of town. He could have been crushed, but the driver chose to turn and broadside him with the length of his truck to even the impact and not hit head-on. Glen was thrown against the driver's door. The air bag helped, his seatbelt helped, but he got a concussion and a broken arm and badly bruised leg. He's a lucky man, Deb. He could have been killed."

Deb had been standing but had to sit. "Thank God," was all she could say.

"Yes," the doctor answered. "You may be with him now. He'll be sleeping a lot due to the concussion and medication we gave him to prevent swelling of the brain. The left side of his face is bruised and swollen and will bruise more, but the discoloration and swelling will go away in time. I tell you this so you won't be alarmed when you see him. Though being a chaplain yourself, you have probably seen it all."

"Yes, but it's usually someone not this close to me. Thank you, Doctor." Deb found Glen in a bed with tubes and machines all around him. He seemed to be sleeping deeply. That was good. She stood by his bed and held his hand and stroked his face. He stirred slightly. "Glen, it's Deb. I'm here. I'll be with you. I love you." His face didn't look as bad as she thought it would. He had a huge bump and a bad scrape on his cheek. His eye was swollen shut and badly bruised. His left arm was broken from hitting the door. It was in a cast. There was a pressure dressing on his leg to prevent more swelling and bruising, but his leg wasn't broken. She stood there studying him. She had seen worse so it didn't shock her. It's more emotional when it's someone you love.

Knowing a person's hearing is sensitive, even when they are in a coma or a deep sleep, Deb kept talking to him and saying his name, touching his cheek. After a while, she sat in the recliner. She cried tears of joy. Everything would be ok. She had to believe that.

She pulled the recliner close to his bed, then left to get a beverage and call Carol back. She could only tell her Glen would be all right. She needed to call his secretary, Barb but it was after work hours. She got her home number from information. She told her everything she knew and asked that she notify anyone she thought would want to know.

When Deb came back, someone had brought her a pillow and blanket. She read for some time and then, holding his hand, fell asleep.

People were in and out all night, checking machines and taking his vitals, asking if Deb needed anything. Toward morning, he started getting restless, moaning and mumbling and tossing in the bed. The drugs were probably wearing off as he was allowed to wake up more. Deb held his hand and talked to him, saying anything so he heard her voice and feel her touch. He was less agitated when she touched him or spoke to him. It seemed to calm him. It was usual for a patient in a coma.

With morning, a stream of doctors and lab people invaded; Chaplain Curtis came too. Everyone assured Deb that Glen did well through the night so he would be allowed to wake up slowly. His condition was upgraded and soon they would move him to rehab. If he continued progressing, he'd need therapy for several days before he was able to go home.

As she held his hand, she planned some options for them. She would take him home with her and convince him to be married right away, so it would be right for him to stay with her while she helped him. One of her pastors could marry them at home. They already had applied for their license, it just needed to be signed and notarized. The church ceremony in three weeks would be a marriage blessing. Besides, Deb wasn't willing to waste any more time waiting to be married to this man. I only hope he'll agree. *Well, I'll just have to talk him into it when he is able to handle it. I'll just wait until he is up to it. In a few days, he'll be able to talk about things.*

Glen began to stir, so Deb kept repeating his name and touching his face. Finally, he opened his good eye. "Deb?" He asked softly.

"Yes, it is, Glen." She leaned close to his face and squeezed his free hand. "Can you hear me?"

"Yes, Where am I? What happened?"

You were in an accident, Glen. You're in the hospital"

"Yes, a truck, hit me," he remembered. "I've been dreaming about it."

Yes, it did. You remember but you're going to be all right."

"I couldn't get out of his way." He stopped. "He came right at me."

"I know. It's all over now, Glen. You're ok. That's all that matters now." She touched his arm to calm him.

He insisted on talking about it. "Why, what happened? I moved over, out of the way but all I remember is the sound of glass, metal, then quiet."

She tried to tell him. It might help. "I didn't talk to the patrolman who was at the scene, but the doctor said a truck was coming down the ramp onto the interstate and his brakes failed. He knew he was going to hit you, so he tried to sideswipe you instead of hitting you head-on. By doing that he saved your life. You're going to be fine, dear. Just rest now. You have a broken arm, a bruised leg, and a concussion, honey. It could have been worse but you're going to be fine."

She cried and hugged him sitting close enough to hold his hand.

He whispered again, "Deb."

"Yes." She stood back up so he could see her.

"I love you."

She kissed him. "I love you too. Rest now. I'm here and I'm going to stay here with you."

"Deb," he began. "I probably don't make sense," he mumbled. "Boy, do I have a headache!"

"You can have pain medicine now. Rest now, if you can." She held his hand, while he slept and she made plans. We could be married here at the hospital by one of the chaplains here, or wait until we get him back to home to Grand Island to call my family again and Glen's office. Barb would have the numbers of Myrna's family to call, and she would help me get the word to everyone else in the cities. Deb had made a list of people to call and get numbers, etc. She went outside for some air and make her calls.

Glen slept for several hours. The next time he woke up, he was more alert and his pain medicine had been increased to make him comfortable. Deb told him so. He squeezed her hand. "The best pain medicine for me is having you here with me. Thank you for being in my life." Deb squeezed his hand back. He stopped. "I thought for a while there that our romance was going to end."

"Me too!" Tears came just saying it. "Glen, you can't get rid of me. Don't even think of it. The best thing you can do now is sleep it off."

"Come here so I can see you" He pulled her hand to him.

Deb hugged him the best she could. "Are you sure you want to be saddled with a cripple?"

"I'm sure. Now shut up and sleep."

"But."

She reassured him. "I thought we'd made that clear when we talked about our feelings and intentions. I want you just the way you are, however that is."

"But Deb, this might change things. I may not be able to do the things we planned. What if I can't..."

Deb put her fingers over his mouth and didn't let him finish. "Don't even go there. Now, you rest. You're just agitated as you try to clear your mind. Don't try yet. It will come in time. I'll be here. We can talk later. You sleep now. You just got some medicine to make you relax so relax, don't fight it." She kissed his face and sat close by so they could hold hands. He slept for a couple of hours again. Deb read her novel and dozed at times. He began to stir and moan. The nurse came to check vitals and his IV.

"Could he be having pain?" Deb asked her.

"Probably, I'll check to see when he last had meds," she said and left.

It was now the second day since his accident. His room was filling with flowers and cards. There were several calls from the guys at work and his secretary, Barb. His pastor, Deb's kids and Myrna's all called. Everyone was concerned, happy to hear he was doing well. Deb gave them all her cell phone number so they wouldn't disturb Glen but could talk to them if he was alert.

Deb came back from returning some calls."Deb, I need to

talk to you." Glen startled her by speaking. She thought he was sleeping. She stood close so he could see her with his one good eye. The other one was still swollen shut and turning purple and blue. "Deb, I've been thinking. I need to talk to you about this, about us."

"Ok, what about us?"

"I think we should put off our wedding. I think we need to wait, ya know, wait 'til we know how I turn out." He had a hard time using the right words. He searched her face.

She got close to his face, kissing him as she said. "I thought I would lose you, before I even had you. You not only aren't going to get rid of me that way. I've been thinking too and my mind is more clear than yours. But I don't want to talk about it until your thoughts catch up with mine."

"I'm just fine. I know what I am saying. Deb, we have to wait, longer, 'til…"

"No," She interrupted again, "I have two options for you. Getting rid of me isn't one of them. We can be married earlier, here and now or at my house when you get out of the hospital or on our wedding day"

"Deb, are you sure you want to do that?".

"I'm sure I do." Then she searched his face. "Glen, have you changed your mind about us? Would you rather not get married at all?" She pulled her hand away from him sinking into the chair beside his bed. "Why don't you take another nap? Sleep on it and we'll talk about it later." This was no time to argue. She needed to calm down and he needed more time to wake up and make sense. He will think more clearly when he gets off the pain meds. "Tomorrow, Glen."

He started, "Deb."

Deb shushed him up kissing his mouth. "Later." She whispered.

He was quiet for a while, his eyes shut. Deb thought he was sleeping, then he spoke.

"Deb." He lifted his head. "Oh, you are still here."

"Yes, I'm still here. I'm not leaving until you can go home with me."

"Deb, I need to talk to you. I've been thinking about what has happened here. We don't really know what my recovery will bring. I might be disabled, at least for some time. All the things we talked about doing together. Our hopes and plans, Deb, everything is different now. We've been able to talk about everything and anything before. Can we talk about this?" He stopped. "We shouldn't rush into..."

Deb took several deep breaths, "we shouldn't rush into this conversation." She needed to give herself time so she would say what needed to be said without losing it. "What are you saying, Glen? That hit on the head, it must have affected your heart."

"Deb, we need to be practical, sensible. We need to think about the future, what this might mean."

"What does 'this' mean?"

"The way things are now, everything is changed. Our lives may be different than we thought and planned." He took a deep breath, wondering how to say it..

She stood up and looked at him. "What has changed? Tell me."

He reached for her and caught her arm. "We need to think this through, not rush. Our wedding, our honeymoon may have to be postponed. Who knows how long?"

"Glen, I'm going to go for a while. You need to rest, without me here to harass. And I need to calm down. Sleep, love." She kissed him and left. She decided she needed a motel room to relax and shower, get a good night's sleep. For now, she went for a walk, found a little gift shop and wandered through it. She bought an iced tea in the cafeteria and went back to say "good night" to Glen.

Deb came back to Glen's room. He was sleeping. She told the clerk at the desk that she had checked into a motel and would leave soon. She made sure they had her number. The clerk shared that Glen would be moved to rehab in the morning so she might want to check his room number. She went back and waited until Glen woke up. Then she told him she was going to a motel for some rest. She would see him in the morning. She kissed him well, saying she loved him.

"Deb," he started. Then he just said, "I love you too. Go rest."

Deb rested well, ate some breakfast and went to Glen's room in rehab with a coffee. He smiled, "good morning. Didi you rest?"

"Yes, I did." She kissed him. Now they will put you to work."

"I have rehab four times a day. Some will be evaluation before I leave but I am doing well. I feel more positive today."

"Good!"

"So can we talk about us today, Deb."

"Here you are, hardly enough strength to speak and you are trying to argue."

"I'm trying to make sense to you," he paused. "To me too."

"Let it go, Glen. This is not the time to make decisions about us."

"But it keeps coming into my mind and then I want to talk about it. I just think we need to postpone our wedding until I am well."

Deb pulled away from him and crossed the room to shut the door. She came back to his bed and began in a low direct tone, "This is insane, talking to you when you're not making sense but here I go." She took a deep breath. "You shut up and listen to me!" Standing over him, she let him have it. "YOU came into my life. YOU made me love you. YOU swept me off my feet. YOU were the one in a hurry to be engaged, get married. YOU, you're the one who couldn't wait. I had to meet your friends so they would become my friends. It's your fault I love them now and want them for my friends too. YOU met my family so they would know you and love you so they would approve of our life together. I was the one at first who wanted to wait to make sure that this was what we both wanted forever, as long as our forever will last. I assumed that meant 'til death do us part'"

He just lay there at her mercy. His eye got bigger as he took it in . "Your noble talk about being willing to take care of me if I got sick because you love me so much. Was that just to impress me? Didn't you mean it at all?"

She didn't wait for him to answer choking a sob. "All of

that was fine as long as it was you caring about me. Maybe nothing would change if it were me lying there instead of you. That's different, huh? If I were lying there, would you want to change our plans, start 'thinking' about us?" She took a deep breath and swiped at the tears streaming down her face.

"Deb…" He tried to stop her. He was crying too."It doesn't mean anything is changed..."

She went on."We have talked about love, different kinds of love, loves of our past, loves to wait for, even love we had to let go of. This thing we call love we professed to each other. Love isn't an issue here, huh? Now, you say we need to think, be sensible. Do you want to postpone our marriage, our life together? Or do you just want to call it all off? Maybe you want to get out of it all together. What do you want?"

"But there is more than love to consider." He protested.

"Certainly, a car accident changes everything. This love of·ours can't withstand a car accident? How shallow!" Deb choked, swallowed, and started again. "Mr. Jarvis, you were willing to take me as I am. But I'm to 'think' about my love for you. I might not want some crippled man."

"Deb, please," he protested. He put his free hand to his head. "I have a headache. I need to think, clear my head."

⊰ CHAPTER 32 ⊱

DEB CRIED "YOU'RE RIGHT. I'M SORRY for my outburst.
Guess I got going and couldn't stop. I'm going to leave for
a while and let you rest. You won't get any with me here
screaming at you. I love you always. Be back soon. The nurse
has my cell phone number and knows where I am staying.
Get some rest, work hard in rehab. We will talk later and I
won't be angry."

She made some more calls. While she waited to buy a
bowl of fruit in the cafeteria Chaplain Curtis walked up.
"Looks like someone could use some company. Just say so if
I'm wrong."

"No, you are right." She told him her story. She was going
to apologize to Glen when she went back up to his room. She
told the chaplain she didn't know if she had lost him or not.

The chaplain assured her that these things take time.
Between his injury and the meds, he was confused. "Give it
time. I bet he is thinking more clearly already. As he heals,
he'll be more positive. Rehab will be helpful. They'll wear him
out and he will sleep and not have time to think so much.
Besides, by now, he is realizing what you mean to him.

Glen lay thinking of all she'd said and his head ached worse. The nurse brought him a pain pill and rehab came for him, making him walk with crutches all the way. They worked his leg and shoulders. He gave up the crutches for a cane.

Deb was waiting in his room when he walked back. "Wow! Look at you!" She said, waiting for him to sit before she kissed him. He sat in the recliner now. He didn't look pleased though. "What. Glen?" She dreaded what he would say.

"I deserved it, Deb, what you said. Was it yesterday? I'm all mixed up on time. My head is still not very clear." Glen looked away. "But you were right."

"Glen, I want you as you are, right now. I finally learned that's what love is. It took me forty years and a new man in my life, and now I know. You are all that I ever hoped for. You are my chance for love and happiness. And now, if you want me to 'think' about it." She stopped, Needing to blow her nose..Glen blinked and tears streamed down his face. With a fresh tissue, she wiped his face too.

She was sorry she had attacked him, especially when he was in no shape to defend himself. Deb wanted to beg his forgiveness, throw herself at him, but she couldn't. She tenderly wiped his face as she cried. Her thoughts were racing, trying to figure out what to do or say next. But her heart was breaking. Had she given her heart to a man to have it given back unused? Had she learned to love completely, the way she thought she could only dream of. She had laid herself bear before him. She felt like such a fool, having been taken in by another man. Maybe it was all a mistake from the beginning.

Perhaps she should have gone for a romance or just plain sex and never gotten involved so deeply. She should have known. Now, she stood there searching his face. She loved him and wanted to marry him. She should just leave but wanted to say more.

"Oh, God, Deb, I don't know where to begin. I've hurt you so. I think my brain is scrambled from this hit on the head," he whispered, reaching for his head.

"Oh, I shouldn't have done that to you. I'm so sorry, Glen. I should have waited until you were stronger, feeling better, able to defend yourself at least. I'm so sorry for talking to you like that, I thought maybe I could shock you into thinking differently."

"I deserved it. I know that now. It isn't my head. It has nothing to do with my head." He searched her face.

Her voice softened now. "It has everything to do with your heart, Glen"

"I was thinking of what was best for you. If I can't give you that." He stopped.

"What is best for me, Glen?"

"I want your happiness. I want you to know you are my happiness."

"Do you think love is just what you can give me? Is all the giving on your part? What about my love?"

He twisted. "I need to lie down". She helped him to his bed, rolled it up a bit and wiped his tears.

"I loved you so much, Deb. I never even thought of how much you loved me. I was wrapped up in my love. It just satisfied me that you loved me at all. I'm sorry, I was so selfish and thoughtless." Then he stopped. "What can I say?"

"Prove you love me and trust my love for you. You have a choice. Either you are in my life all the way to stay, no matter what, or just leave me alone."Tears streamed down her face. "Well, what will it be? Now or never."

"Deb, I think, I don't..."

She cut him off, saying softly, "Love is in the heart, not in the head. There is no reasoning or thinking. We either love each other or not."

He started laughing. Deb felt the anger again. How can he laugh now?

"What's so funny? I don't see anything funny here." She walked to the window but was crying, so she couldn't see out.

"Slow down, woman. I'm not laughing at you, but am amazed at your words. I want you to be on my side whenever you have a strong opinion about something. You come on like blockbusters. Come here, will you? Please?"He stopped. "I can't come there."

She walked back to his bed and just stood there glaring at him. He tried to search her face for a way to reach her. "Don't scare me like that. That look on your face. It breaks my heart to see that look of hate or anger. What is it? I've never seen you like this"

Shaking her head, she said "It's not you, just shades of the past. You can't make it all better by offering words, Glen. I need to see the action that follows. Oh, I have said all I will. It's up to you." She stood in silence.

Glen started to speak slowly. "I was scared to death that I

would lose you. First because of the accident and now because of my foolish pride. I just didn't give you any credit for loving me as much as I did you." Then continued. "Okay, you gave me two sets of two choices. You said 'now or never.' I'm choosing now."

Deb threw herself at him. He hugged her as tightly as he could with one arm. He began again."Then you said we'd be married here or at your house. I don't know how long it will be before I'll be released from here but Deb, I would wait until we get to your house if you like. That would be nice."

"Glen. I was afraid I'd lose you too. First to an accident and then to the words spewing out of my mouth. I was trying to convince you with words. I was sorry I said those horrible things. After all, you did have a hit on the head. I could have waited until you had a chance to get well but you kept pressing."

"I am glad you did say what you did. It took that to make me realize what love can do to people, how desperate they can get when they think they might lose it." He held her close with his good arm and kissed her forehead. "I never want to take that chance again. Now I know your love for me and I know I never will lose you."

"Glen, I promise I will never talk that way to you again."

"God, I hope not. I feel like I've been through a battle."

"You have, my dear, more than one in a matter of three days." It was so quiet now; the only sounds were in the hall outside.

❈ CHAPTER 33 ❈

DEB CALLED HER PASTOR AND GLEN talked to him. He said he would make all the arrangements for the marriage ceremony at Deb's as soon as they were ready. He said they would need a civil license to make it legal. Glen told him the status of that.

Glen had three or four sessions a day in rehab walking and strengthening his shoulder. He did so well, he even went without the crutch. The last day, his strength and ability were evaluated. Being physically fit was paying off. He was able to push himself to his capacity without much fatigue. He was a model patient, grateful and gracious, and he kept his sense of humor. Watching him under stress helped Deb to realize what a strong person he was in every way.

The fifth day, Deb went to the business office and got the things that had been in his car. The Buick had been totaled. He wouldn't have to sell it now. Glen was loaded into the back seat of Deb's van and they left for Grand Island. They talked some and he rested some. Deb tried to help him into the house but he stubbornly wanted to do his own thing. He sat at the table while she fixed soup and a sandwich. Then she took him into her bedroom and ordered him to take a nap in her virgin bed.

"This isn't right," Glen argued with Deb. "It's your room, your bed."

Seated on the bed, Deb pulled off his shoes, and laid him down, covering him with a warm comforter.

"No one has ever slept in it but me," she whispered to him placing pillows around him. "Think of how privileged you are. It's no longer mine, but ours from now on." She lay down beside him. "There are no more yours and mine. It's ours from here on." She snuggled close to him on his good side.

"This isn't exactly how I planned the next few weeks," Glen apologized.

"Me neither, it's turned out better than our plans, except for your owies."

"Yeah, it could have been worse. I still have reruns in my head of the accident and what followed."

"You will for a while," she remembered an accident many years ago.

Glen pulled Deb close. "God, I could have missed all of this," he whispered. She didn't answer knowing he was just thinking, perhaps praying out loud. After a few moments, he went on, "Losing my life was one thing. Being gravely hurt, leaving me grossly impaired. That's another. Then..." his voice caught. He stopped. "I was willing to give us away because of the possibilities of..."

Deb interrupted. "We'll chalk it up to the bang on head. You weren't thinking clearly, Glen." She kissed his head. "You can't get rid of me, no matter what you do. It's too late for that." Flashing her ring in front of him, she added, " you made a commitment to last forever. Not only are we getting married, but we're being married sooner than we planned." She sat up, facing him ready to cry. He took her hand, pulled it to his heart. "This is our last night with rooms and bedclothes and other things between us. Tomorrow is the day. Tomorrow night we will be one."

"So where will you sleep tonight when I'm in your bed?"

"In my bed, I'm sleeping in my bed even if you're in it… a night early."

"But, what about our urges, my desires, what…?"

"I'll count on your disability to stop you from taking advantage of me."

He laughed, "Don't count on it." He kissed her.

"I think I can handle you in this condition. Wouldn't it be fun and naughty though if at our age we couldn't wait and had premarital sex? Ooooo!"

"Deb, you are a nut and an eternal optimist. You see the blessing in everything. I wonder how we will do things like go on our honeymoon with me like this and you.."

"I think it will add to the adventure, for sure. Honey, we'll make it one."

Deb sat up. "Now, you rest awhile. I have things to do." She brought Glen's bags into the bedroom after he woke from his nap. He got up and unpacked his own clothes into a couple of drawers she'd emptied in the dresser. He wanted to "do something."

Pastor Thompson stopped by in the evening to discuss what would happen the next day. He also needed to "give them marriage counseling, a crash course," he said. He would return at one o'clock tomorrow. Deb's daughter Peg and her husband Ron would be witnesses. Deb ordered a catered lunch and invited the church staff to make it more festive.

The Pastor prayed before he left. "Heavenly Father, you truly are a father who watches out for your children. You have proven that by taking care of Glen through his accident. Grant him healing and freedom from pain. Bless him and Deb and their love as they take a sidestep in their life and plans. You, dear God, are truly in charge of our life and life events. Bring us to know your care, and trust that your plan works best. We pray this in Jesus's name, Amen."

Glen took a final walk before getting ready for bed. He still insisted on taking care of himself. He said he felt like it and needed to get stronger. As he crawled into bed, Deb tucked pillows around him. "Are you sure you want to sleep with me and my stuff?"

"I'm sleeping right here with you. You can never get away from me again. But do you mind if I stay up awhile?"

"If you have to. You won't make a habit of this, will you?" He teased.

"No, but I've been gone for several days, so I need to do a few things. Besides, I'm not tired yet. It's only nine o'clock. You need your rest. I don't yet."

"Ok, but waken me when you come if I'm sleeping."

"I thought you'd be tired, ready to sleep. It has been a long day for you. You can turn on the TV for a while."

"It has been for you too, Deb."

"Yeah, you're right, but I may not sleep tonight anyway,

having a bed partner after all the years I spent alone could affect my sleep."

"Me too, I hope." He stopped. "Is that why you want to stay up, to avoid going to bed with me? Deb, I didn't expect this."

"Not at all, Glen." Sitting beside him, she took his hand. "No, I just thought you'd be ready for some sleep. Are you having any pain? You have meds if you need them."

With his free hand, he cupped her face. "I know this isn't what we'd planned, but I want you get your rest. Let me use your guest room." He started to sit up.

She pushed him back down. "No, you stay here. I'll get ready for bed and lie here with you for a while, and if I don't sleep, I'll get up, ok? Would you like the TV on?"

"Hand me the remote." She went into the bathroom to clean up putting on her flannel PJs, not intending to get too alluring. She locked up the house and brought two mugs of hot chocolate. Then she crawled in beside Glen, snuggling for a few minutes.

He assured Deb she was "safe" tonight. He was tired..She wasn't worried, but a little disappointed. They watched the evening news and M*A*S*H. Then turned it off. Deb was so excited about having him here beside her, even in his wounded condition but she slept anyway.

She opened her eyes hoping to get a glimpse of him sleeping beside her. Glen was laying there smiling, watching her. They lay in bed, talking and snuggling for a while. Deb put on a robe and helped Glen get his cast covered so he could shower. He insisted on dressing himself as much as possible. One problem was finding a way to put shirts over his cast.

T-shirts weren't so bad. Deb split the sleeve of one shirt and jacket, and sewed Velcro on the seams. She'd do a few others if needed.

Flowers were delivered. Deb had ordered a single rose for Peg and herself and boutonniere for Glen and Ron. Secretly, Glen ordered a dozen roses.

The food came ready to serve. Peg and Ron came and Peg set the table for lunch. She brought a small wedding cake.

Pastor Thompson brought Jan and Lila from the church office. Since Lila is the office manager, she is also a Notary so could witness the signatures on the civil marriage document. Deb had the tree up and decorated so the Christmas tree served as background for the ceremony. It was short and meaningful. The important part was being married in the bane if Jesus Christ.

Pastor warned them that he would tell this story in a homily at the celebration in the church. When everyone left, Deb suggested Glen take his nap. He accused her of wanting him in her bed. She agreed, and the sooner the better. "Really, Mr. Jarvis, don't you feel like you need to rest for a while?"

"Mrs. Jarvis, I just want to be close to you. I'll lie down but I don't want to sleep, ok? I'm too excited. I just got married, you know!"

"Me too! What a coincidence!" They rested awhile and then Deb did a few things that were on her mind while Glen went through his exercises.

Life fell into days of getting ready for Christmas. Glen did what he could to help. In fact, he even learned how to maneuver his damaged limb. He sat on a stool and stirred candy, the kids' favorites, caramels, fudge, divinity, and toffee. He figured out a way to one-handedly put cookie dough on the trays, chocolate, peanut butter, molasses, and he even decorated sugar cookies. He packed them in containers. He really was a lot of help, but mostly it was fun having him there. They laughed a lot, just getting used to each other's ways. He also had a lot of people to contact.

Bedtime was wonderful. Now they could lie in each other's arms and talk. They took their time making love. The only restraint was Glen's injuries. He could see from both eyes now and his leg still looked bruised but worked. The local orthopedic doctor changed his cast to a brace. It was softer so not such a handicap both bathing and love-making. Being careful only made love better. Except for the first night, it was hard to hold back when they were both so hungry to satisfy pent-up desires. "I never realized how much I needed love 'til now. I mean the mad, passionate part." Glen confessed.

"Me too, scary huh but wonderful," she shared. "Glen, I hope I didn't scare you."

"No, my dear, you were wonderful. I was worried that I might not be able to satisfy you." He lifted his arm, "especially with this."

"Mmm, you satisfied me." She pressed her face into his neck. "Very much. Wonder what you'll be like when you get rid of your handicap,"

"Remember when you told me about the four kinds of love?" Glen asked.

"Yes."

"I know this is Eros Love. But Deb, you told me about Agape Love, or C. S. Lewis's view, do you remember?"

"Yes, well, I'm not sure what I told you but you fell for it."

"Well, you said it is love that forgives completely and cares for others above all, especially self. You said we can try to achieve agape love, but we are usually too human to accomplish it. I believe I have this is perfect love." He choked back his emotion. " The beautiful part is that I love everything about you. Your perfections, your faults, I never want to change any part of you. I have never known love like this before."

"Nor I. You put it so well, so right. This love is a special love, God's gift to us. I don't believe I deserve it. I can't believe it is happening to me, but it is."

❧ CHAPTER 34 ❧

As WORD GOT AROUND ABOUT THEM, the mail increased. That and Christmas cards, it was fun to see whom they'd hear from each day. He even insisted on walking out to the mailbox. With a blanked of snow, he used a cane for safety.

The house and food were ready. Deb was packed for their honeymoon trip and had sorted out stuff enough so the kids and grand kids could take the things they wanted and could pick out other items she no longer wanted to keep. Two days before Christmas, the kids and grand kids began arriving. They stayed at Deb and Glen's with the overflow at Peg's. Deb always enjoyed the whole bunch together at once, and Glen ate it up. He hadn't had so much family ever. Christmas Eve, everyone went to church, taking up two pews. Gifts were opened afterward until midnight. Deb's gifts to her family were keepsakes. But Glen had bought a gift for each one of them. He bought pendant necklaces for each of the gals. For the guys, he'd gotten gift certificates at a hardware lumberyard.

There were the usual fun gag gifts for each other. It was a tradition for many years and might seem strange to most, but Glen thought it was delightful. No cost was spent chosing treasures from thrift stores and and garage sales throughout the year.. Santa came during the night. A lot of elves contributed to the stuffing the stockings.

Son, Jay and grandson Jacob came for the three days around Christmas, but Jay wouldn't be able to stay for the wedding. His band was booked for holiday parties, so he flew out on the twenty-sixth. But he had chosen the "privacy" of family for Christmas instead of the wedding crowd as his time to be with family. It had been several years since he'd been home, and in fact, since the whole family had been together, so Jay really enjoyed it. Jacob stayed and was going back with the other kids

❖ CHAPTER 35 ❖

AT LAST, MARRIAGE CELEBRATION DAY, THE thirtieth arrived. It took one person just to answer the phone. All of the females went to the church and hotel to decorate, while Glen and the guys relaxed in the hotel lounge. Dan, Jr. was impressed that all the guys had a beer, but Glen refused, not wanting to smell of booze at the church. Dan told his mother about it. They'd planned for Dan to walk his mother down the aisle, so he felt protective of her..It was good for him to have that role. He needed to feel like the head of the family. His approval was important.

Peg and Carol were beautiful as bridesmaids. Deb was as proud of them as they were of her. Glen's nephews, Paul and Curtis, grown men now, with families of their own completed our joint family. Deb hadn't seen them since they moved away from Mallory thirty years ago. It was fun getting to know them and their mom, Connie again. She came with her second husband, Walt. Several friends even came from Mallory. Only one couple from the Twin Cities, friends of Glen, were unable to come. The couple were grateful for their support.

The blessing at the church was at five, so everyone left by four o'clock. The church filled with guests.

For the ceremony, Pastor Thompson told Deb and Glen's story well with humor, since many church members might not know it. He told how they had met thirty years ago and now again so recently. He used scripture to remind each of us that God's timing and sometimes conflicts with ours, that, His time is different from ours. Now, God was blessing us with time that would be to our advantage as we shared the time we had left in our lives to be together as one. He reminded that these events and the timing of them are never a coincidence. Our guests could see that we were willing to take that risk and live life to the fullest.

From the sacristy came Glen's friend, Pastor Hanson from Central Lutheran. They didn't know he was going to be there, let alone be a part of the ceremony. He shared the story of an anonymous elderly monk who wrote a letter late in life:

"If I had my life to live over again,
I'd try to make more mistakes next time.
    I'd relax, I would limber up, I would be
Sillier than I had been this trip.
    I know very few things I would take seriously.
I would take more trips. I would be crazier.
    I would climb more mountains, swim more rivers,
And watch more sunsets.
    I would do more walking and looking.
I would eat more ice cream and less beans.
    I would have more actual troubles,
And fewer imaginary ones.
    You see, I'm one of those people who live life

Simply and sensibly hour after hour, day after day.

Oh, I've had my moments, and if I had it to do over
again

I'd have more of them.

In fact, I'd try to have nothing else,

just moments, one after another,

Instead of living so many years ahead of each day.

I've been one of those people who never go anywhere

without a thermometer, a hot-water bottle, a gargle,

a raincoat, aspirin and a parachute.

If I had it to do over again I would go places,

Do things, and travel lighter than I have.

If I had my life to live over I would start barefooted
earlier

in the spring and stay that way later in the fall.

I would play hooky more.

I wouldn't get such good grades, except by accident.

I would ride on more merry-go-rounds.

And I'd pick more daisies."

⚜ CHAPTER 36 ⚜

PASTOR **D**AVE CONTINUED, **"I** BELIEVE YOU, Deb and Glen, have done many of these things, already in your lives. Now, you have each other to spend the rest of your lives riding those merry-go-rounds and taking walks and picking daisies. You have learned what is important in life and what isn't. God places these opportunities in front of us and expects us to grab them."

He called them brave and exciting people for taking advantage of an opportunity to share life and faith with each other and those around them. He said that in spite of a minor setback in the last month, they turned into a blessing of the gifts of life.

He prayed: "You are blessed to replace loneliness and aloneness with a special love that pours out to each other and encompasses those around you. It is here now and we all feel it with you."

Deb began crying softly and squeezed Glen's hand. He pulled his handkerchief out and blotted her tears. "Thank you" She whispered. Then she looked at him and he too was crying, so Deb took his handkerchief and dried his tears too. It sounded like the congregation swooned.

Pastor Dave said, "See!" Now people were laughing and whispering.

Taking a seat in the first pew with their attendants, they sang with the congregation "He Leadeth Me," one of Deb's favorite hymns, and Glen chose "Oh, Master, Let Me Walk with Thee." Special music that had been planned as a surprise was grandchildren, two of Glen's and six of Deb's, singing and playing piano, guitar, and drums. They performed a "youthful version" of "Joyful, Joyful We Adore Thee."

Pastor Thompson reminded the guests that Glen and Deb had already been married when Glen got out of the hospital. So at this was a time of sharing the blessing of marriage. As they kissed and walked back up the aisle, everyone cheered. No one waited to be ushered out. First the grand kids jumped up and followed them, and then everyone else.

Dan announced after the blessing that anyone wanting to leave his or her car at the church and ride to the reception could just wait here for the limousine and that there were two handicap vehicles waiting for those who preferred. They would also have a ride back to their cars when they were ready. The limousines filled with kids first. As soon as guests were seated in the hall, Glen prayed the table grace. Deb was so proud of him. After the meal, cake and ice cream were served while they roamed around, visiting with everyone.

✄ CHAPTER 37 ✄

THE INFORMAL PROGRAM WAS FRIENDS AND relatives telling stories about Glen and Deb and wished them blessings.

Glen at last could share his news. They stood and he said, "Now, what Deb has been waiting for, where we are going on our honeymoon." With that cue, an officially dressed travel agent came to stand before them and announce the places and events to take place soon. She had brochures and maps. "January 1, you leave Grand Island, flying to St. Paul, then on to Hawaii for one week. From there, you fly to Tahiti for another week, boarding a cruise ship to New Zealand and Australia. Points of interest throughout the islands end with a flight back to Hawaii, and then to San Francisco to rest from jet lag. The month long trip ends back in Grand Island." She finished her professional speech with "Why you would want to come back to the north in February is beyond me, it's up to you to keep warm your own way." She was embarrassed, having said it. Everyone cheered and laughed.

By the time the program and toasts ended, a DJ was set up and ready to play for the dance. Deb's son, Jay had pulled strings and arranged for him since it was short notice and most Djs were booked this time of year. He also refused to let us pay him. Jay did. Glen and Deb danced the first dance together. In fact, it was the first time dancing with each other in over thirty years at another wedding.

The newly weds tired before most of the others, so they sat and visited, enjoying watching young and old having a good time together. Soon the limousines started taking people back to their cars. Deb and Glen gave up by midnight as did most guests who would be leaving for home the next morning. Family and friends would be leaving tomorrow and packing up their treasures to take along.

Deb finally had her dream of traveling to the South Pacific coming true and she had Glen to do it with. Glen seemed to know what would please her.

❧ CHAPTER 38 ❧

THE TRIP BEGAN WITH HONOLULU, HAWAII. It was as beautiful as Deb had imagined. She'd never been there; Glen had, so he knew the places he wanted to share with Deb. The first night, was romantic watching the sunset from their balcony. The next morning, they enjoyed luscious fruits and breads for breakfast on the patio watching the sunrise over the ocean. The breezes blowing the scent of azaleas and orchids toward them.

As they looked out toward the beach, enjoying the view, there was a group of people waving from the beach. Being friendly, Deb and Glen waved back. The whole group, eight or ten of them, came closer. They continued to wave and began to call to their names; at least that is what it sounded like. Finally, they were close enough to recognized them. It was Glen's friends from the Twin Cities, ten of them. They came to join the honeymooners in Hawaii. They decided they'd had enough time alone already, so they needed friends to party with.

"Surely we were bored being alone with each other by now," his friend, Jim said. They were kind to leave them alone at night, but it was wonderful going to luaus and beach parties, and sightseeing with them. For those who were able, mountain climbing, biking, rock hounding, and swimming in the ocean were great with them.

One thing some did that Deb always wanted to do was snorkeling. The vibrant colors of rocks and coral and the schools of fish and sea life were unforgettable. Glen's friends, now Debs friends, treated her as if she had always been one of them. Time and again, they shared how wonderful Glen was and how much happier he was now. Promising to travel together again, and talked about adventures they'd share next. They flew home as Deb and Glen continued their trip.

This isn't the end of our story. But that is all I will tell, as I remember it "all over again."

❧ END ❧